SMITTENED

PIPPA GRANT WRITING AS

JAMIE FARRELL

Cover Illustration by Julie Bonart of Qamber Designs
Cover layout & typography by Qamber Designs
Editing by Penny's Copy Sense

*M*ikey Diamond lived large. He worked hard, he played hard and now, apparently, he burned hard.

His house sure did, anyway.

Sirens rang out, red lights flashed in the night and the acrid taste of smoke choked him. Worst part was, that burning fire hadn't done a dang thing to warm up the cold January night.

Or it might've been his own conscience causing that bitter chill under his skin.

"You think they'd let us close enough to roast marshmallows?" a feminine voice said beside him.

He blinked down at a curvy woman with an upturned nose. She pushed a pair of glasses back up said nose, then squinted at the fire. "Good thing it's vacant, huh? I wonder what started the fire."

Mikey looked at the burning two-story structure lighting up the night. Then back at the lady.

She was vaguely familiar—he and Will had been in town a few days and had met a lot of people—and Mikey was all but certain his momma would label her one round short of a full clip, then probably toss a *bless her heart* on top of it.

"That's my house," Mikey said.

She drew back and squinted at him. "No, it's the—*oh*. Oh."

Ding-dong, the lightbulb had entered the building. "Yeah."

She shot a glance around. No doubt looking for Will, Mikey's best friend and travel companion, known to the world as country music superstar Billy Brenton. In other words, the more interesting of the two of them.

Also, the one who had just left Mikey here to fend for himself with no transportation and no shelter. Not that Mikey could blame him.

It was Mikey's fault the house was on fire. And while Mikey had lost a suitcase of clothes and a computer, Will had lost a little more.

A hell of a lot more, matter of fact. Better Will was gone, or he might've tried to go into the fire after it.

Mikey shuddered.

The girl shifted a speculative glance in Mikey's direction. What was her name? Something with a D. Delaney? Delilah?

"So…" she said.

Mikey treated her to a slow grin. Not because he felt like it, but because she was wearing loose pants and clunky slipper shoes under her coat, because he'd never minded using his status as Billy Brenton's drummer to his advantage when it came to women, and because she obviously knew the neighborhood.

Which meant the girl most likely lived close by.

She probably also had a car nearby and could give him a lift to a hotel. And a lift was all he was up for tonight, which might've said something about how badly rattled he was at seeing the house burn down. Because Mikey was *always* up for *something* when it came to women.

Except now, apparently. "So?" he prompted.

She visibly swallowed, nose wrinkling as though she'd drank curdled milk. "So… you're still sticking around Bliss?" she asked.

It was Mikey's turn to taste that milk. If it were up to him, he'd be on the first flight back home to Georgia.

But he was here in Illinois—in the Most Married-est Town on

2

Earth, God help him—to keep an eye on Will, both for his own peace of mind and as a favor to Will's sister, Mari Belle. Mikey wasn't leaving until his buddy did. Given what Mikey knew about *why* Will was here, neither of them would get gone until either Will solved his love life, or until the next leg of the Billy Brenton *Hitched* tour started next month.

"Yep, sticking around awhile," he said slowly. What *was* her name? Dixie? Darla?

"So you need"—she visibly gulped—"a place to stay?"

Mikey opened his mouth to say no, but choked on a lungful of ash.

He *did* need a place to stay.

She fluttered her hands at something behind them. "My house is just over there, and I have a spare bedroom, so this is quite serendipitous. Except for the part about your current rental house burning down. That's a little unfortunate. Obviously."

"Obviously," Mikey echoed. "Unfortunate."

"A tragedy." She puffed up her chest under her fluffy coat. The more primitive parts of Mikey's brain noted that she did, in fact, have a nice chest. Even if covered with infinite layers of polyester. Were they somewhere other than Bliss, he would've noticed sooner.

"My heater works very well," she said. "No frostbite in my house. Did I mention that part?"

"Don't think so, sweet pea. But it's right good to hear."

"Yep. Working heater, and I even cook breakfast. Won't get that at a hotel. You two will have to share a room since I only have one guest bed. Or maybe I could sleep on the couch. You know. I'm flexible. With sleeping stuff."

The normal alarm bells rang out in his head over her assumption that she'd be getting Billy Brenton as part of the package. But the primitive part of Mikey's brain was getting louder too, cheering every time she said *bed* or *sleep*. *Share* was another he didn't mind either. And *flexible*.

But it still wasn't loud enough to distract him from the fire and his concern over Will. Mikey needed to give him a call. Make sure he was okay. Had found a place to stay.

"Billy's making his own arrangements," Mikey said to—what *was* her name?

"Oh." Her lips twitched down, but she beat them into submission and flashed him a semi-brilliant smile with wide, full lips and dark eyes that sparkled with the reflection of the fire. "Pity for him, isn't it? So. Are you coming, or would you rather be a Popsicle?"

He took one last look back at the burning house. Fire chief had Mikey's number and had already said there wasn't much else Mikey could do tonight. Everything inside the house was gone.

"Suppose I can give you a night to impress me." He gave her a slow wink.

"Best night you'll ever have," she said with a naïveté that was almost refreshing. "Best breakfast too."

Probably not, but he'd take what he could get.

DAHLIA MALLARD HAD LOST her ever-loving mind. But desperate times, desperate measures, blah blah, all that. She'd already sold plasma twice this week, and while she had gotten a bid on the eBay auction for Great Aunt Agnes's vintage Christmas Story Leg Lamp, she was running out of things to sell.

Selling herself might very well be next, and by the looks of him, Mikey would be willing to pay.

He looked much more harmless in Billy's weekly BillyVision YouTube videos than he did in person. Less wolfish. More all-talk, less follow-through.

She twisted her doorknob and suppressed a shudder. This would've been easier if Billy were here too. Aside from the part where he'd struck her mute when she'd run into him and Mikey earlier simply by being *Billy Brenton*, he was so approachable. Plus, he sort of had connections here in Bliss, indirectly, and Dahlia had heard he was "good people."

And since she'd totally choked during her chance to ask Billy for one teensy little favor when she met him, Mikey needing a place to stay tonight truly was serendipitous.

Serendipitous.

Right.

Sheesh.

Mikey wasn't *serendipitous*. He was a giant vibrating mass of pheromones, oozing masculine power and control as though he converted oxygen into testosterone instead of carbon dioxide.

And he accomplished all that simply by breathing. Ducks only knew where her clothes would end up if he spent much time brandishing that deep Southern drawl for anything beyond asking where she kept the toilet paper.

Or if she thought too long about the haunted look in his eyes when she'd found him out there watching the fire.

Haunted and lost, as though he needed to be saved.

Nope, she wasn't going there. Had enough of that, thank you very much.

She was only offering him a place to stay in the hopes that he could help her make a miracle.

She swung her door open, put on mental blinders to his raw animal magnetism, and led him inside. "So this is—Parrot! Bad kitty! Shoo! Shoo!"

Parrot, her black and orange tortoiseshell rescue cat took off at a run for the bedrooms, leaving the tampon she'd been playing with lying in the middle of the floor. Dahlia would've kicked it under the couch, but she'd sold that last week, and now a green-striped easy chair was the only furniture on the expanse of matted tan carpet in the living room.

Plus her glasses were fogging and she couldn't exactly see it clearly.

Still, she swooped down, located the tampon, and shoved it in her pocket before Dean and Sam, her orange tabby and gray tabby, respectively, could dart in from their spots on either side of the chair for their turn with Parrot's toy. Dahlia's glasses slowly cleared, revealing Dean playing with a tennis ball, lying on it and scratching at it with his back feet. Which made it look more like the cat was humping the ball than playing with it.

"Right," she said, turning to force an *all good here* smile at Mikey, which was a mistake because it meant looking up at those haunting gray eyes that were tracking her from beneath the brim of the ball cap covering his shaved head.

Seeing everything. He still hovered in the door, silhouetted in the flash of red lights and the residual glow of the fire across the street. "Real nice chair you got there," he said. One corner of his mouth tilted up, and Dahlia got the distinct impression she'd just been asked to take her clothes off. "It fit two?"

Six months ago, she wouldn't have fought temptation.

But six months ago, she hadn't yet met Ted, and he hadn't yet *borrowed* her life savings. "Of course," she said. "The cats will be happy to share it with you."

His corner smile dropped. He pulled his cap off, ran a hand over his smooth head, and took another glance about the practically empty room before shoving the cap back on.

Dahlia practiced her yoga breathing and tried to slow her racing heart. She truly didn't want him to stay—she was *so* done with charity cases, losers, and playboys—but she couldn't pass up the opportunity to seek Billy's help through a proxy.

It wasn't as if she wanted to ask him to strip for charity. She simply needed him to sample some special ice cream and tell a few—hundred—people about it.

She wanted to howl. She'd turned into the kind of person who usually took advantage of *her*.

But The Milked Duck needed help, and she'd be failing all the little kids of Bliss who spent their summers stopping in for ice cream treats if she had to close the shop because she went totally broke this winter.

"The kitchen's stocked for the basics; the spare bedroom has clean sheets; and there's plenty of hot water. And you could definitely use a shower. *Phew*."

Those gray eyes slid back to her. "Your shower big enough for two?"

"Yes, but the cats don't like to get wet. Neither does the guinea pig. But you might have some success with the lizard."

Bad, bad move. Because *both* corners of his mouth were getting in on the smile action. He moved them one at a time, first the right corner, then a slow follow from the left corner.

And then he showed his dimple.

Trump card every time.

Ducks, she was a mess.

"Whose lizard?" he said.

"My iguana," she clarified, intentionally ignoring his *you want to see my lizard?* eyebrow wiggle. "Hank. He's a rescue, an old boyfriend left him here, but he's a total sweetie. Would you mind closing the door? The cats shouldn't be out when your house is burning."

His cheek twitched, and he eyeballed the chair again, where Dean had paused in humping the tennis ball long enough to join Sam in eyeing Mikey back. But Mikey stepped all the way into the house and shut the door carefully. The red lights still flashed through the front window, and the hint of smoke would probably linger inside for days, but the bigger problem now was having this tall mass of hot, unfiltered maleness alone with her in her house.

No doubt about it.

She was sleeping with her bedroom door locked tonight.

"You can help yourself to anything in the fridge," she said. "But the freezer is on the fritz—every time it's opened, there's a humidity imbalance that makes the defroster malfunction and leak all over the floor. So if you could leave the door shut, that would be awesome. I can probably treat you to an ice cream cone, but you'll have to come down to the shop tomorrow to get it. I don't bring the goods home from work or I'd weigh like eight hundred pounds."

Lying wasn't her favorite pastime, but she hoped the visual would make him quit eyeing her as though *she* was the ice cream cone, and that her flimsy reasoning was enough to discourage him from snooping in her freezer.

"Right," he said. "You're the ice cream lady."

She sucked in a lungful of courage. "Yeah. I have this tasting going on Saturday after next. It'll be—" Fun? Sexy? Her last chance at solving her money problems? "A great time. You should come."

Mikey shot a glance at the chair again as if he hadn't heard her. "The ice cream lady with a zoo."

"With a home," she corrected.

And, apparently, with the gift of being too subtle.

Or he recognized the invitation to the flavor tasting as a personal favor she had no right asking, and he was ignoring it.

She was *so* not good at asking for help.

She gave him a quick tour of the kitchen, which didn't take long considering it was as minimally stocked as her living room.

Only the necessities. Everything else had been sold to pay last month's rent.

Two years ago, she had inherited The Milked Duck Ice Cream Shoppe in downtown Bliss from Great Aunt Agnes. After getting her degree in sociology and then bouncing around the country, waffling from job to job and one relative's couch to another, she'd finally found where she fit: creating and serving happiness to the locals and the destination wedding tourists in Bliss. Two winters ago, she'd learned the importance of saving summer profits to survive the slow winter months, because even perpetual weddings and the smell of love in the air didn't bring people in for ice cream as often in the colder months. This year, Dahlia thought she had everything under control, but then Ted happened.

Swooped in and stole Dahlia's heart. They talked for hours about animals, about ice cream, about Bliss and its Knot Festival and weddings. Because one couldn't move to Bliss and *not* talk about the primary function of the quirky little town. And then Ted had shared his passion for books. He was an academic with both a love of the literary and an analytical mind, and so he'd decided to launch a book recommendation service online. Because there were *so* many books to choose from in the digital age, he said.

He'd been so smart about all of it—the Internet, the market, the method of determining which books were the best to recommend to the reading public. He simply needed capital to invest in building the Web site and newsletter. Because graphic designers were expensive, he said. And people wouldn't take his recommendations if he didn't look like he knew what he was talking about, he said. And he needed money for marketing to get start-up attention, he said. And then, with the income stream from affiliate programs and the paid advertising from authors, Dahlia's investment would make itself back threefold in a matter of weeks. It all made brilliant sense.

And because Dahlia was a fool, she had loaned him the money.

It had been three months since she'd heard from him. Two months and three weeks since his cell phone had been disconnected.

She had to make it only to May. Just another four or five months. Then business at The Milked Duck would pick up again. She'd be super smart this time, and everything would be fine.

Until then—she'd figure out a way to get Billy to her risqué flavor tasting event.

She watched Mikey poke in her refrigerator—the only thing well-stocked in her house—then eye Hank in his cage in the corner, and then survey the rose-print wallpaper and original 1950's cabinets in the little house Dahlia rented.

Living at The Milked Duck would be a smarter option. She could save a lot of cash while she waited for summer to roll around if she put a sleeping bag in the corner of the kitchen.

Except then she'd have to find temporary homes for her pets, because they couldn't live with her at the shop. And surrendering their care to someone else for an indeterminate amount of time simply wasn't an option.

Once Mikey was done in the kitchen, she led him back to the bedroom. "And this would be your room," she said, trying desperately not to look at the bed dominating the otherwise empty room—taking a roommate was one of her ideas to save cash—or to think of him stripping out of his clothes, or to think of him sliding his naked body between the rose-colored satin sheets—who was she kidding?

She could *so* use a romp to let off some steam. And he looked as though he could help her let off a *lot* of steam.

Except Ted hadn't been the first guy to take Dahlia for a ride. So she was off men. Even men who presumably had money in their bank accounts. And who weren't making any false promises of staying. And who were eyeing her cats again as though they could infect him with a fatal case of fleas simply by looking at him.

"Looks mighty comfy," Mikey said with a nod at the bed.

Dear sweet holy ducks, that husky note in his voice might make her orgasm on the spot.

She backpedaled out of the room. "So I'll let you get comfy. Breakfast is at seven-thirty."

"Wait," he said. "Two quick questions."

No, waiting was bad. Waiting with him using the *I want to lick you like an ice cream cone* look on her was worse. "Yes?" she said.

He dangled his phone in the air. "You got a spare charger?"

"I'll leave it on the counter in the kitchen."

"Thank you much, sweet pea."

Sweet pea. It should've been so demeaning. But her impressionable little heart happy-sighed. He'd given her a nickname.

One he probably used on every other pulse-bearing female on the planet, but her heart had never been the best judge of character.

"And your other question?" she said.

"Yeah. That other question." He flipped his ball cap off, ran a hand over his smooth head again, then put the hat on backward. And if she'd thought she was getting the ice-cream-licking smile before, she got a triple-scoop-with-caramel-fudge-and-a-cherry-on-top whopper this time.

She may have whimpered.

He tucked his hands in his pockets. "I, ah," he said, "forgot your name."

Of course he had. Self-absorbed country rocker band guy. Why would he need to remember little old Dahlia's *name*?

Still, Dahlia's wretched sense of self-worth wanted to reach out and pet him. Offer up a *That's okay, honey. You had a bad day.*

Except that's what the old Dahlia would do, and the new Dahlia needed to command some respect. She cocked her head and smiled back at him. "That's a shame. It's well worth remembering. I recommend meditation. It helps improve memory function." She let her gaze drift south. "Among other functions. Sleep well. I'll see you in the morning."

And the new, improved Dahlia Mallard marched down the hall to her own bedroom, where she shut and locked her bedroom door, then collapsed in a heap like the hot mess that she was.

*M*ikey didn't sleep well. Being in Bliss, the fire, the feisty, curvy lady with the glasses and the red streaks in her dark hair whose name he *still* couldn't remember—it kept his mind humming and his body wanting *something* to take the edge off.

Sleeping with his hostess wasn't an option. One, while he rarely declined female attentions and ministrations, he *always* knew their names. And two, he didn't do opportunists. She'd swooped in mighty fast with her offer of a place to stay. She had an agenda, and he suspected it had to do with her ice cream tasting.

He was used to being asked for handouts, and even more used to seeing people ask Will for handouts. Like all the guys in the band, Mikey was good at deflecting the requests. But he'd been freaking cold outside, and worse, he'd been alone.

Mikey wasn't big on being alone.

Which brought him to the third, and probably biggest, reason he wouldn't sleep with his hostess. She wasn't Mari Belle. Most nights, he could get past that, but tonight, Mari Belle was on his brain.

Mikey's first memory of her was of her standing over him and Will, a stringy-haired doll in hand, lecturing them about being more careful where their Hot Wheels were flinging mud. Irritated him then, made him smile today.

He remembered one spring afternoon hanging out at Will's Aunt Jessie's house, tossing a baseball with Will, throwing it way off the mark when Mari Belle walked out of the house in a fluffy pink prom dress. When Will had heckled him about the throw, Mikey asked when Will's sister had turned into a girl.

Pretty girl at that, though Mikey hadn't said it aloud.

Then Mari Belle going off to college, bringing a boyfriend home. Getting engaged the Christmas before she graduated. Coming home after spring break that year, the year she'd dragged Will along, and coming to see Mikey before she had to head back to college.

He'd been sure she'd come to tell him she'd broken things off with the guy, but no.

She'd said Will got his heart broke on their trip. Got his heart tore to shreds, matter of fact, and Mikey would be doing Mari Belle a big ol' favor if he kept an extra close eye on her brother.

Would've done it anyway, but he liked having a reason to talk to her.

About tore his own heart to shreds watching her get married though.

Mari Belle, she had a plan. And she'd done it. Got the college degree, got the job, got the husband. Then came the baby. Everything she'd ever wanted, hers forever.

Didn't have room for Mikey, so he went on and found the next best thing.

All the next best things.

Once he and Will hit Nashville, Mikey got popular with the ladies. Enjoyed his life a hell of a lot ever since, even if he did battle being lonely from time to time.

And then Mari Belle got divorced.

Mikey thought he'd had a chance with her once or twice, but as soon as he worked up the nerve to try something, he chickened out.

Every time.

Only secret he'd ever kept from Will.

Will, his best friend.

Just last week, Mikey had promised Mari Belle—again—that he'd look out for Will, since Will was here in Bliss because the girl who tore him to shreds fifteen years ago was here too.

Will had texted earlier to ask if Mikey had a place to stay tonight. When Mikey had answered that he was set and asked the same in return, his buddy had ceased communication. Now, Will's phone was rolling straight to voicemail. No surprise—everyone from his manager to his publicist to a million other people with a stake in the Billy Brenton empire would want to know their lead man was okay. Mikey caught some rumors on Twitter that he'd been spotted at a store in the next town over. Mikey had also called Mari Belle. Good to hear her voice, like always, but would've been better if it hadn't been because Mikey had let Will down.

Let them both down.

The fire chief had said they wouldn't know the cause of the fire until the fire inspector came out, but he'd been willing to lay odds it was the space heater Mikey hadn't turned off.

So with all that in his mind, Mikey rolled out of the bed in the otherwise empty room around 2:00 a.m. He pulled his clothes back on —he'd showered and gone to bed naked, but his smoky jeans, shirt, boots, and jacket were all he had to his name here in Bliss right now— and then ventured out of the bedroom in search of a snack.

House across the street was dark. No more flashing lights.

Just…empty blackness.

Mikey rubbed his arms and went on to the kitchen. The freezer was loaded down with ice cream—so that's why his hostess didn't want him inside it—and despite the lack of furniture in the house, Mikey thought he might find a piece of paper.

Couldn't sleep. Might as well write a song.

That sparsely furnished thing bothered him. So did the zoo, but he had an inherent distrust of cats. Getting on out of here first thing in the morning was a dang good idea. Had a friend of a friend he could call for a ride to get a rental car if Will was still hiding, and then Mikey would get himself some new clothes and a hotel room and wait out his buddy.

He helped himself to a carton of something called—he squinted in the low light glowing over the range—*Chocolate Orgasm?*

His having an orgasm over chocolate ice cream was about as likely as the creek back home running whiskey instead of water. Still, he dug a spoon out of a drawer, popped the top of the plain brown carton, and dug in.

Chocolatey goodness coated his tongue. Not too sweet, not too bitter.

Pretty dang good, actually.

He took another bite, and went poking in the drawers for a pen and pencil. Like the living room and his bedroom, the kitchen was stocked enough to be livable. Weren't enough plates and cups to handle the masses; barely enough other stuff to heat up a can of soup or fix up a plate of spaghetti.

Mikey had played in Vegas long enough to know when to take a bet, and he was betting his hostess was having some money problems.

Her lizard in the glass tank in the corner stared at him, making judgments on Mikey for making judgments on Lizard Boy's mama.

He'd seen some weird stuff during his days on the road, but this was high up the list.

Should've stayed in a hotel. Still could. Quick phone call would get him a taxi.

Instead, he pulled out the drawer on the other side of the dishwasher and found what he was looking for. Kind of.

There was a small pad of blank paper and some pens, but he had to dig under some consignment shop receipts to find it.

And maybe it was the Chocolate Orgasm ice cream mellowing him out, or possibly he was nosy, but he pulled out the receipts and looked closer.

Dahlia. Her name was Dahlia.

And it appeared that she'd sold near about everything that should've been in her house.

"*Mrroowl?*"

He shuffled the receipts back into the drawer. The black and orange cat that had been playing with a feminine product when he walked in was circling his legs and rubbing on his pants.

"Ain't happening, cat," Mikey muttered. He took the pad of paper to the long counter that jutted out under a row of cabinets between the kitchen and the dining room. Wasn't a kitchen table to sit at—she'd sold that for two hundred bucks last week, her receipts said—but he'd written lyrics in worse conditions.

Eaten a lot worse ice cream too. Stuff was killer. In the good way. Not orgasmic, but still killer.

He bent over the paper under the cabinets, scribbled a line.

The cat jumped up on the counter and walked between him and the paper, flicking its tail at his nose. He gave it a nudge. Then another nudge. On the third nudge, it finally moved, and he went back to tapping his pen on the paper. Somewhere else in the house, another cat yowled.

They went on like that for a while, Mikey writing, the cat butting in, Mikey pushing it away, other cats making a racket.

"What are you doing?"

Mikey jumped. His head collided with something solid, and a piercing pain shot through his skull. "*Ow! Shit!*"

"Oh, ducks," she muttered.

Mikey blinked and clenched his jaw shut. Damn cabinets.

Soft fingers landed on his shoulder. "Are you okay? Is it bleeding? Do you need ice? Wait—*are you eating my Chocolate Orgasm?*"

Suddenly the fingers were gone, and so was his ice cream. "That's a prototype," she shrieked. The red streaks in her hair stood up on end, and her face morphed into angry clown mode.

He didn't much like her right now for having a house with cabinets he could hit his head on. He rubbed the sore spot where a knot was already forming. "You might could think about putting bumpers on those things," he said.

"You *might could* think about not being an ice cream stealer," she shot back. "*Argh*. You ate the whole thing!"

"Begging your pardon, *ma'am*, for not knowing which of the seventy-eight cartons were off-limits."

Uh-oh. There went the freeze-ray eyeballs. She could've directed them to his head to help control the swelling, but nope. They were aimed right at his nose and more likely to be turned onto his private parts than to be used for any good.

Women.

"They're *all* off-limits," she said in that *I will kill you and chop your body into a million pieces that I will store between my seventy-eight cartons of ice cream* voice. She punctuated her statement with a thump of the empty carton.

He strolled back around the counter and went to the freezer. Because he wanted ice, and she was pissing him off, and if there was one thing he was good at, it was pissing right back. "Chill, lady. It's just ice cream." He flung the door open, grabbed the next container he saw, and put it right to the sore spot on his head.

She made a noise like a feral animal, and darned if the cats at her feet didn't stop circling to look at him and hiss too.

And suddenly he had no more ice cream in his hand, he'd been unceremoniously shoved halfway across the kitchen, and she was shrieking a lecture at him like—well, like Mari Belle had when he and Will had borrowed her nail polish collection to paint lines for their short-lived underground armadillo racing venture when they were nine.

Turned out armadillos weren't so easy to catch, if you could even find the live ones.

He tuned back in to Dahlia's shrieking in time for the grand finale. "And you're an entitled, selfish, thoughtless jerk."

He held his hands up. "Now slow on down there, Ms. Opportunist—"

17

"Oh, don't you even—"

"I don't know what you want from me, but I ain't staying in a death trap."

"It wasn't a death trap until *you* were dumb enough to bend over under a cabinet. How long have you been over six feet tall? Did that happen yesterday? Last week? Still getting used to your height? Please. Your being a klutz isn't *my* fault."

Damn female logic.

She had a point.

He was the problem.

"Here." She shoved a frozen gel pack at him, and the anger shooting off her mellowed. "Are you feeling dizzy? Nauseous? Any numbness in your extremities?"

"What, was there something *special* in your ice cream?" he said like an ass.

"Estrogen," she said. "You might notice some swelling in your boobs and shrinkage in your package for a few days."

He straightened and almost hit his head on the cabinet a second time. "*Wha—*"

She tipped her head back and laughed, and Mikey *did* get a little light headed then. "Shit."

Her laughter slowed to giggles, but then she looked at him, and darn if that smile of hers didn't go bigger. She laughed again, this time with her shoulders getting into the action, scrunching up toward her face while she rocked forward and let the laughter overtake her.

Definitely feeling the effects of hitting his head.

Because watching her laugh—that was a darn near beautiful sight.

He put the gel pack to his head, felt a smile of his own creeping out. "You ain't funny."

Her gray cat gave him a *don't-be-a-dumbass* look, then bent over and licked its privates.

"I'm very funny," she said, still giggling, her cheeky grin making her skin glow and her dark blue eyes sparkle.

She was wearing a Rolling Stones T-shirt as pajamas, he noticed.

Nice. Good taste.

His eyes drifted lower.

Black pajama pants with bright red lips.

His crotch twitched.

Trouble, he reminded himself.

But, hey, he knew her name now. That eliminated almost half the problem with sleeping with her. Not the bigger half, but knowing her name made him feel less like an ass. "You having money issues?" he heard himself say.

All her amusement died right quick, and she went stiff as a dead armadillo in springtime. Her skin paled to the color of snowflakes, making two freckles on her left cheek stand out starkly. She shoved her glasses back up her nose. "First you eat my ice cream, then you insult my house? Starting to see why Billy left you."

Defensive. He was right on. Had some smarts in him every now and again.

Wasn't so sure it was smart to want to know her story, though. Didn't like to let the girls *too* close. Arm's length was his usual MO. "Everybody struggles sometimes," he said when he should've kept his trap shut. "Should've seen how me and Billy lived before we hit it big in Nashville."

Her claws retracted. Not all the way, but enough for him to see she was softening to the idea that he wasn't out to kick her while she was down.

He liked her softer. Looked more natural on her.

"Winter's slow for an ice cream shop owner," she said.

"You sell your furniture every winter to get by?"

Her eyes narrowed again, and he was honestly surprised she didn't hiss and take a swipe at him. Her orange cat looked to be wanting to do the same. "I have everything I need, thank you very much."

"Got a boyfriend?"

She grimaced.

Bingo. "He stole your cash, huh?"

Her jaw dropped. "How—why—"

"I'm a songwriter, sweet pea. Always looking for the good story."

"You—you're—*argh*."

He was. He was *argh* with himself too. Wasn't always looking to get pissed on a lady's behalf—he'd done that plenty for Mari Belle, and that hadn't ever got him anywhere—but the thought of somebody doing Dahlia wrong had Mikey wanting to hit something.

Girl could use her tongue to slice a guy up, but the way she hugged herself made him think she wasn't all that tough. Maybe a little lonely too.

He propped his hip against the counter and grinned at her. "Go on. Grab another carton of ice cream and tell Uncle Mikey all about it."

"You're a dirty old man."

"Not yet, sweet pea, but I'm working on it."

She shook her head. "C'mon, Parrot. Dean and Sam, you too. Let's go back to bed."

Another flash of lonely welled up and threatened to choke Mikey. "Might could help you find out what's wrong with that Chocolate Orgasm. Was missing something."

He was missing something. Was called his brain. Needed to let the lady go.

But she cocked an interested brow at him. "Was it now?"

"Some fudge," he improvised. Because the ice cream had been dang near perfect.

She studied him a minute, all dark blue eyes and well-deserved suspicion. When he thought she'd turn around and walk away, though, she popped open the freezer.

Mikey leaned forward.

She dug through the cartons and came up with one from the back. Then she grabbed a fresh spoon, popped the top off the carton, and gave him another speculative look.

"Fudge," she said.

She scooped out a heap of the chocolate ice cream and lifted the spoon to his lips, her deep blue gaze holding him captive. He opened his mouth and hoped if she happened to look down, she wasn't the type to throw a man out in the cold just because being fed by a woman was a lesser-known personal fetish.

So few women knew how to do it right, but Dahlia was a pro. Her own lips parted as she slid the spoon into his mouth, and Mikey went from half-mast to fully charged. He closed his lips, hers pursed shut, and she pulled the spoon back out. At first, all he tasted was cold, but then chocolate cream trickled over his tongue.

Chocolate cream with a hint of spice and a rich, full burst of pure chocolate heaven. His eyes crossed, then slid closed.

Yeah.

This was the stuff.

With sweet chunks of brownie and fudge and something crunchy.

His taste buds were definitely having an orgasm.

He had to grip the counter behind him to keep steady.

If the woman could do that to him with a spoonful of ice cream in the dead of winter, there was no telling what else she could do.

He opened his eyes.

She was watching him, her arms wrapped around her middle, still holding the spoon and the ice cream. Her eyes flickered—curiosity, uncertainty, desire?—but otherwise, she was completely still.

Waiting.

Mikey cleared his throat. "Don't know, sweet pea. Gonna need another bite or six to tell you what's missing."

Her lips pursed, eyes narrowed. But then she flashed him the sweetest, brightest grin he'd seen all night, and his heart went thumping like a bass drum in a dance song.

"It's a good thing you talk," she said, "because otherwise, you might be attractive." She tossed the spoon in the sink, then swung her pajama-clad hips on around and sashayed right on out of the kitchen.

And she was taking the ice cream with her.

"Hey, wait—"

"You can consider the ice cream your breakfast," she said over her shoulder. "Thanks for your help. I have to get to work."

And before Mikey could get control of all the parts of him that had shut down during his chocolate orgasm, she disappeared.

Smart man would've thought that was for the best.

Mikey, though, was already planning on staying here another night.

---

3

*B*y lunchtime, Dahlia was tired but happy. After she'd recovered from watching Mikey's reaction to the Chocolate Orgasm ice cream, she'd picked the final recipe and now had her whole menu set for her adults-only risqué flavor tasting event, her last-ditch effort to increase sales at The Milked Duck this winter. So far she'd only sold about six tickets for the tasting, despite passing out fliers to all the businesses downtown, but she had a Knot Fest subcommittee meeting tomorrow. She'd volunteered to help Natalie Blue plan the Husband Games, and Nat had a lot of influence around town these days, so Dahlia was hopeful Nat could help encourage people to sign up.

Getting Billy Brenton to come, though, would pack the event. But even if Dahlia could find the nerve to ask Billy, rumors were that he was deep in hiding after the fire last night. Which meant Dahlia's best bet for getting to him was still Mikey.

He made her nervous.

Not because he was scary. But because he was so danged intriguing.

Dangerous, all things considered. Dahlia wasn't interested in saving a playboy from his womanizing ways. She needed to save herself first.

The doorbell dinged out the ice cream truck song that Great Aunt Agnes, rest her soul, had installed shortly before she kicked the bucket. Two years, and Dahlia still couldn't figure out how to change it to a normal ding. She popped up to the front of the store to take care of her customers.

Except it wasn't customers.

It was Mikey.

She braced herself and girded her loins, which, quite honestly, needed a *lot* of girding.

Especially when he aimed that smile and those gray eyes at her. He strolled over the black checkered floor, all lanky grace and undeniable sensuality in his leather jacket, cowboy boots, omnipresent ball cap, and new blue jeans. "My favorite ice cream lady," he said.

Her heart squeezed. *Charmer*, she reminded herself. And not even a good one at that. "You say that to all the ice cream ladies you meet."

"Not anymore." He winked and propped his elbows on the glass counter over the tubs of ice cream. He lifted a suggestive eyebrow. "Was hoping to try some of that Cherry Popper ice cream for lunch."

"What—how—who—*Hush!*" No one was supposed to know anything on her adults-only menu until the tasting. Which meant he'd been snooping more in her house.

The only thing more annoying than the smug in his smile was the way her pulse fluttered in response to it.

"Saw a note," he said casually. "I'm a big fan of cherries."

"So you've said a couple hundred times," she muttered.

He peered closer, his grin spreading wider to show off a row of perfectly aligned pearly whites. "Why, Miss Dahlia, you've been watching BillyVision."

He knew her name.

Oh, sweet holy ducks, he knew her name. It sounded so exotic in his Southern drawl. *Daawl-ya*.

"Well, yeah," she forced out. "Billy's hot."

His smile went bigger, and for the first time since last night's fire, she noticed his eyes crinkling at the edges too. "But I'm better."

Yes. Yes he—no. No. She didn't need to add *philandering pig* to her list of dating disasters.

"I guess," she said. "Sort of like the mashed potatoes that go with the Thanksgiving turkey."

The ego in his grin didn't waver. "So you want to cover me with gravy? I might could be up for that."

That was not an image that should've been sexy. Chocolate syrup, yes. Warm caramel sauce, absolutely. Lumpy brown gravy on Mikey? Ducks help her, it was not totally revolting. She stepped back from the counter and grabbed a rag to wipe at an imaginary ice cream dribble. "You should probably stick to playing music," she said. "Not sure you could do the gravy justice."

"Sure I could, sweet pea. I'm a man of many talents."

No denying that. He could probably make *I plugged your toilet and flooded your bathroom* sound sexy.

"Speaking of talent, how's Billy today?"

If she hadn't looked, she would've missed the quick brow-furrow and dip in his smile. The smug *I-am-a-sex-god* look came back quickly, but not quickly enough. "Not near as good as I am," he said with another wink.

Dahlia ditched the rag to snag a small ice cream cup and a scoop. "Has he found suitable accommodations?"

Mikey ducked his head, but not before Dahlia caught the growly face overcoming his *I'm-too-sexy* act.

Holy ducks again.

He *was* acting. Using his overt sex appeal to hide his worry over Billy.

No. No, no, *no*. She was *not* getting involved.

But she was dishing up a small scoop of Chocolate Cherry ice cream, which was nothing next to the cherry bourbon Cherry Popper she had stashed in back, but unless Mikey was offering up Billy as entertainment for Dahlia's adults-only tasting, he didn't get any Cherry Popper.

"You two have been friends a long time, haven't you?" she said, exactly like an idiot who was getting involved.

He eyed the ice cream offering. Then her. Then the ice cream. "My whole life," he said.

With none of the swagger, none of the ego, none of the *let's do the horizontal polka* innuendos lingering in the tilt of his lips or the waggle of his brows.

Like he was a regular guy.

Don't go there, Dahlia.

"You're worried about him?" She set the cup on the counter beside him. He glanced at it, then looked back at her once more, his gaze searching, serious.

There was a storm brewing in the back of those gray eyes.

The man was more than he let the world believe. And that was a dangerous, dangerous realization.

He dropped his gaze and snagged the ice cream. "He's working through some stuff. And ice cream ain't enough to make it better."

Dahlia leaned closer into the counter. "What kind of stuff?"

"Ain't my place to talk about it."

Which meant either he really didn't want to talk about it, or he was afraid Dahlia would mention it to one of the reporters snooping around town. Not that any of them were interested in stopping in a little ice cream shop on a side street in downtown Bliss on a blustery winter day.

Mikey, though, took the ice cream, holding the cup between his thumb and forefinger, looking for all the world like he *wanted* to talk about it.

Like whatever was wrong with Billy was wrong with Mikey too, but he couldn't talk about his own struggles for fear of betraying his friend to tongue-waggers and gossips.

She still shouldn't go there. Mikey was a player. A man-slut. A master at performing.

But he looked so sad.

And Dahlia had never been able to resist sad. "I let my ex have my life savings to invest in a book recommendation business, but it was all a scam," she blurted.

Mikey turned those gray eyes on her while he licked his spoon.

Her thighs clenched.

"Sweet pea, you're about the cutest mess I've ever laid eyes on."

She was such a dingbat. "And you're very gullible," she said. "I was trying to make you feel better because you looked sad."

He took another bite of ice cream, and his eyes slid half-closed.

Her heart joined in a little of that throbbing that kicked up between her legs. Mental note: No more watching Mikey eat ice cream.

Wait.

No more *giving* Mikey ice cream.

"How long did you know him?" Mikey asked.

"I didn't. Know him. I was joking."

"Two weeks, huh? Had that coming."

"Three months," Dahlia said. "And my family met him and liked him too, and they're all very good judges of character." They were all horrible judges of character, but they were all saving the world in their own ways—her sister at a horse sanctuary in Montana, her parents on a mission in West Africa—and Dahlia couldn't justify complicating their lives with her little problem. Not when she could solve it herself.

"You let him move in with you right away?" Mikey said.

"No, he had his own apartment."

"And a job you never saw him at?"

"He worked in Willow Glen. It wasn't exactly easy to pop by to visit him at his office for lunch. It's half an hour each way, not including eating time."

And now she was defending herself to a guy who really didn't care and who was only using her to make himself feel better about whatever his own problems were.

She was *so good* at this interpersonal relationship thing. "You need to leave," she said.

He didn't budge. "You call the cops?"

"I *gave* him the money. I can't call the cops to report my own stupidity."

Crap. She was going to cry. Right here, in the middle of The Milked Duck, which was worth a crap-ton of money if what she paid in property taxes on it was any indication, and which she couldn't afford to keep even though she loved it more than she'd ever loved anything she'd done in her whole adult life.

"Please leave," she said.

But he still didn't move. Didn't step back, didn't even go for another bite of ice cream.

Instead, he stood there watching her fight back the lump in her throat and the sting in her eyes, his head tilted, eyes serious and crinkled in thought. "You see the good in people," he said.

"Yes, yes, I'm a fool. Go away. The ice cream's on the house."

He set the cup on the counter. But when she thought he would reach for his wallet, instead, he brushed his thumb over the moisture that had found its way to her cheek. "World needs more heart," he said.

Her heart pitter-pattered. "More idiots to prey on," she muttered.

His lips tightened. He dropped his hand, and this time he pulled a money clip out of his back pocket.

She stepped back and sucked in a big dose of *get over yourself, Dahlia*. "It's on the house," she repeated. "Because you had a rough day."

"It's good, but it ain't Cherry Popper good," he said.

"Wasn't meant to be."

He flashed her another Mikey grin, tossed a twenty on the counter, and then angled toward the door. "You have a nice afternoon, sweet pea. See you tonight."

And before she could process exactly what all that meant, he'd strolled out.

And she'd completely forgotten to ask him if he and Billy—mostly Billy, of course—would come to her tasting.

———

MIKEY LEFT The Milked Duck and stepped out into the chilly Northern winter. Dahlia's cherry fudge ice cream left a cold trail down his throat and behind his ribs, but it was a delicious kind of cold.

A lot different from the windy cold weather.

And Dahlia not asking him for money when it was obvious she needed it—that was a lot different too.

Girl had him confused and curious.

Nice distraction, he had to admit. But now that he had new clothes and had logged into his cloud account and verified his computer had backed up before becoming toast last night, it was time to take care of the more important stuff.

He hunkered into his coat, his fingers aching from the cold, but instead of jumping into the rental truck he'd picked up this morning, he walked around the corner onto the main downtown thoroughfare, eating his ice cream.

The Aisle, locals called it. Lined with bridal boutiques, jewelers, florists, bakeries, and other specialty shops—anything a couple could need to plan a wedding.

Made Mikey shrink in certain important appendages. Wouldn't go near The Aisle if he weren't wanting word from Will, whose phone was rolling straight to a message that his voicemail was full. Before calling the big guns—Will's management team—Mikey decided to check in with a few locals who might know where he was.

He braved a bakery filled with wedding cakes and one of those bridal boutiques full of white fluffy dresses and brides-to-be, but he struck out on finding word of his buddy.

Either Will had left Mikey stranded in a freezing cold place that had a massive wedding cake monument guarding one end of its down-town, or this little town's gossip express didn't run on the same tracks that Pickleberry Springs' grapevine did. Back home, everyone and their grandmother not only would've known where Will was, they would've worked out a complicated plan to fool any outsiders looking to guess.

On his way back toward his truck, his phone rang.

Even though he should've felt some fear at the picture that popped up on the screen, he smiled, then swiped the phone to answer. "Morning, Mari Belle."

He strolled back down The Aisle, phone tucked between his ear and shoulder while he savored more of Dahlia's ice cream.

"Will still isn't answering my calls," Mari Belle said, her voice hushed like she didn't want to be overheard. At the office, Mikey guessed. She insisted on providing for herself, despite what Will offered to do for her, and didn't like to talk about who she was related to in public places. "Probably my own fault," she continued. "Paisley heard me practicing my come-to-Jesus talk when I saw that picture of him and you-know-who last weekend, and I think she tipped him off."

Mikey's private smile went up a half-notch. Sounded like something Mari Belle's ten-year-old daughter would do. Girl picked Uncle Will over her momma every time. "Have to be more careful, MB."

"Oh, shove it, Mikey," she said good-naturedly. "Is he okay today?"

Mikey passed two women on the street. He caught them eyeing him and gave them a wink and the famous Mikey smile. The older one fanned herself. "Couldn't rightly say," he said to Mari Belle.

One of Mari Belle's legendary sighs wafted through the phone and practically created its own breeze right there in Bliss, eight hundred miles away. "You know where he is?"

"Nope." Not for sure, anyway. Had a hunch. Didn't like it. Wasn't about to invoke the wrath of Mari Belle—beautiful as the show may be —by mentioning the possibility either. Mikey glanced back at the women he'd passed, but they'd stepped off the street. "It was my fault the fire started." Fire chief had confirmed it a little bit ago. "I left a space heater on."

"Well, neither of you got hurt, and that really *is* the most important thing," she said. "He'll get over—oh, mother stuffer. Where's her house?"

Mikey didn't answer.

Partly because while he knew who *her* was—the only girl Will had never gotten over, despite what she'd done to him, and the woman Mari Belle had asked Mikey to protect Will from—and partly because he didn't know her address.

Yet.

"He's there," Mari Belle said. "You find out where she lives, and you go talk some sense into his thick skull, or I'm gonna march right on up there and give him a what for until his ears bleed."

Mikey cleared his throat. "Might could be this one needs a softer touch."

And there went another Mari Belle sigh. Mikey smiled again despite himself. Girl could have a whole conversation with just them sighs. One of the things he'd always loved about her.

Possibly Mikey was as big of a dummy about girls as Will was.

Difference was, Mari Belle had always been family, whereas Will's girl had torn him up and spit him out in a week, and the effects had lasted a lifetime.

Mikey eyed the last bit of ice cream.

Might be the kind of ice cream worth getting torn up over.

Which was near about the craziest thing Mikey had ever thought.

"Still like to see you up here," Mikey said to Mari Belle. "Might could go light on giving him the what for though."

"He needs to get himself back on home."

"Sure enough, but he ain't going to." Three women his age stepped out of another shop. Mikey grinned and nodded at them, and the shorter one and the blonde smiled back. The brunette tripped on a flower box.

"All okay, ma'am?" Mikey said, holding a hand out to the brunette.

"I'm good," she stammered.

Mari Belle's chuckle echoed in his ear. "You don't ever quit flirting, do you?"

"Living the dream, MB." Since he'd never had much hope of having her, he'd had everyone else. "Y'all be careful now," he said to the trio. "Hear tell the sidewalks are slippery in winter."

He treated them to another Mikey smile and a wink, and kept on walking.

"Good ol' dependable Mikey," Mari Belle said. "You call me the minute you find him, you hear?"

"I got this." He winced. "No more space heaters, but I got this."

He turned the corner, and caught sight of The Milked Duck sign hanging off a wrought iron bracket over the ice cream shop's door.

That Dahlia—she was a whole other kind of crazy. Intrigued him more than a normal amount, that was for sure.

"I'm pricing plane tickets," Mari Belle said. "I don't think I can swing this weekend, but next is looking good."

Mikey's heart kicked into its normal seeing-Mari-Belle rhythm. "Give a holler if you want a ride from the airport or anything else."

"I'm a big girl, Mikey. I've got this."

Yep. Stubborn and independent. That was Mari Belle. Stubborn, independent, and overprotective of her brother, her daughter, and her aunt.

Overprotective of everyone but Mikey. "Yes, ma'am."

They hung up as Mikey reached The Milked Duck. He glanced inside. A small group of women sat at one of the cutesy tables now, knitting and eating ice cream. Dahlia was nowhere in sight. Must've been doing her secret things in the kitchen.

He had half a mind to go back in for more ice cream and poke and prod her, but he got the feeling she needed saving more than she needed teasing.

Saving had never been Mikey's strong suit.

So instead, he climbed into his truck, fired it up, and waited for the heater to kick in while he pulled up the Internet on his phone.

He had a best friend to track down.

4

Dahlia got home after closing the shop shortly before five. A black truck was parked in front of her house. After glancing at the charred remains of the house across the street, all she wanted was to change into pajama pants and curl up with her kitties. But inside, she found a one-man band set up in her living room.

Mikey was in the lone chair in the room, chopsticks tucked behind his ear, two five-gallon buckets upside down on the floor beside her upside-down stockpot, which was propped up on a box. Two metal pan lids teetered on the edge of another box. A pretty acoustic guitar lay in an open case on the floor.

He looked up from the paper he was scribbling on and offered her a lopsided grin. "Hey, sweet pea. You bring me anything special?"

The lopsided bit wasn't odd, but there was something forced about it. "Got a fresh bag of cat food outside." Cat food that she'd bought with the twenty he'd left to pay for his ice cream.

He pushed his makeshift drum set aside and rose with a stretch. "Words every man dreams of hearing. Make my night if you say you got catnip too."

She tried not to giggle. She tried hard.

But she couldn't help herself. "Extra strength," she said.

This time, his grin came out bigger, less forced. "Woman of my dreams."

"*In* your dreams," she said.

"Sit on down." He pushed the buckets and boxes aside. "Look like you walked all over yourself without stopping to ask for directions all day long."

"Thank you?"

He took her arm and steered her into the seat, where Parrot promptly appeared out of nowhere to leap onto her lap. Dean slunk in from the kitchen to throw himself at her feet, and Sam yowled from the bedroom.

She smiled.

Home.

"You like pizza?" he said. "I hear tell there's a great place around the corner that delivers."

He was being entirely too agreeable. "What do you want?" she said slowly.

If he was insulted, he didn't show it. Instead, he treated her to one of those smiles that could've evaporated her Chocolate Orgasm ice cream on sight. "Some quality time with a pretty lady."

"All out here." She tried to stifle a yawn and failed. "Might try the next block down. One of the local caterers has twin daughters who recently graduated college."

He didn't even look at the door.

This was getting odd. And not at all comforting.

"You like pepperoni? How do you feel about mushrooms?"

"I'm a vegetarian."

Didn't blink at that either. Instead, he pulled his phone out and thumbed over the screen. "Tomatoes? Peppers? Eggplant?"

"Garlic and onion," she said.

Just in case this was supposed to be a *date*.

He grinned over the top of his phone at her. "Two of my favorite foods."

Yep. She would have to kick him out. Because this whole home-less-but-sweet-and-shameless-and-in-need-of-a-woman-to-save-him thing was hitting *way* too close to what she usually went for in a guy.

"I am *so* not kissing you tonight," she informed him.

He chuckled softly. And if she thought his smile was dangerous, his chuckle should've been classified as a biological weapon. Sin in a sound wave.

"But now you're thinking about what it would be like, ain't you?" he said.

"Only my stupid parts."

"Don't you worry, sweet pea. I got other plans for our mouths tonight."

Images of his mouth on her hand, on her shoulder, on her breast came to mind. Then lower, on her—Dahlia bolted out of her seat, scattering the cats. "Not hungry," she said. "Tired. Bed time. *Sleep* time. Alone. Sleep alone time. Stay out of my freezer. G'night."

"Was talkin' about talking," he said, but there was nothing innocent about his feigned innocence.

She crossed her arms. "Did you see Billy today?"

He winced. It was a quick thing—there and gone, replaced with a semi-bored tilt of his brow, but she knew she'd hit a nerve.

She swallowed the instant apology bubbling up. No, it *wasn't* her business, but if he could push buttons, she could push right back.

"He's still sorting through that personal stuff," Mikey said slowly.

Dahlia hadn't realized her shoulders had lifted, but they sagged in disappointment. She knew code for *He's not interested in being seen in public* when she heard it.

She thought so, anyway. It wasn't often that she was actually one degree away from a megastar. She sucked in a breath, licked her lips, and pushed ahead anyway. Because—well, because why the heck not? What did she have to lose? "Do you think he'd want to come to my tasting event?" she said, sounding every bit the pathetic loser she felt like.

Like a user. Somebody who only cared who these people were because of what they could do for her.

"Might," Mikey said. As if she wasn't asking a *huge* favor of someone she had no right to ask anything of. His mouth hitched up again. "Specially if he gets a sample."

This was entirely too easy. "Is that your way of asking for a three-way?"

He barked out a laugh. "Sweet pea, when I do a three-way, it ain't ever with Billy."

"Oh." Heat flamed in her cheeks. "Right. My bad. I can't even pick a single man at a time. Obviously."

Mikey squeezed her shoulder. "Wouldn't want to share you with anyone anyway," he said softly.

Her heart went warm enough to melt an iceberg. "Don't say things like that to me," she whispered.

So long as he wore his womanizer side, she could resist him. But when he acted like he knew how to use his heart—she was in trouble.

His hand dropped away, and he cleared his throat. "So half veggie, half pepperoni. I'll pick it up. Quicker than waiting." In a wink, he'd flung his coat on and was heading out the door. "Back in a few," he called.

And she wasn't sure if that was supposed to be a reassurance or a warning.

MIKEY DIDN'T DO SLEEPING women.

And he meant *do* in all senses of the word. Didn't touch them, didn't watch them, didn't wake them.

Especially didn't watch.

But when he got back to Dahlia's house with the pizza, she was conked out in the chair, her head tilted into her shoulder, glasses crooked, arms tucked in as if she were giving herself a big ol' hug. A section of her red-streaked dark hair fell across her round, rosy-hued cheek. Even with her lips twitching as though she was dreaming about kissing, she looked fresh and innocent as a snowflake. One cat was in her lap, another on the seat back behind her, the third sprawled across her feet. All three eyed him as though they were thinking of making him their dinner.

Even the devil cats couldn't stop his visions of picking her up, tucking her into bed, kissing her hair, and wishing her sweet dreams.

She took care of people, and they took advantage of her. Wasn't right. Yeah, she was probably using him to get Will to her ice cream thing, but Mikey's visit with Will had confirmed what he suspected: His buddy was staying in Bliss until he'd worked out his past. So to take his mind off Will's problems, Mikey had called an old fling this afternoon, someone who knew how to find things and do things, and had her do some digging.

Not too surprisingly, Dahlia was hanging on by a financial thread.

And there were hints she'd done this before, bailing out other people—at the expense of her own bank account. He was fixin' to hit something if those *people* were all ex-boyfriends.

Girl needed a keeper.

Mikey tiptoed past her and into the kitchen. The lizard eyed him over a plate of lettuce, and two of the three cats were still tracking his movement from their perch in the living room.

Dahlia, though, slept on.

Mikey pulled two slices of pepperoni from the box, grabbed a napkin, and headed back to his bedroom. Because the more he thought about the girl needing a keeper, the more he thought it was his business.

He didn't do long-term. He lived on the road, he had good friends and family who loved him despite his faults, and he never lacked for female companionship. Didn't need to get involved with a small-town girl who kept her own small zoo but couldn't manage her life.

Except Mikey wasn't on the road and he didn't have any friends or family to hang with tonight, which meant hitting a bar was the smartest thing Mikey could do.

Get out, talk to some girls, grab as much normal as he could to remind himself why getting to know the ice cream lady any better was a bad, bad idea.

There was exactly one woman in this world who got to tear Mikey up emotionally, and it wasn't Dahlia.

He paused on his way out the door to drape a blanket over her and the two cats sitting on her.

Yep. Finding some fun was exactly what ol' Mikey needed. So he hightailed it on out of Dahlia's house and over to a little place he knew.

For a bar in the middle of nowhere, Suckers wasn't a bad joint. An hour after he arrived, Mikey was digging the purple mood lighting, the curved steel bar, and the red stools.

He was trying to dig the single ladies crowded three-deep around him, listening to him tell the story of the time he and Billy and the rest of the band played in a freak September snowstorm in South Dakota. Put all the right emphasis on almost losing his fingers to frostbite but putting on the best show for the fans anyway, and the ladies were eating it all up. Petting him, offering to kiss his long-healed boo-boos, doing all the right things to make a man feel worshipped.

Usually everything he wanted out of a night out with the ladies.

But tonight—tonight, he was thinking about soft curves, round rosy cheeks, and dark eyelashes. He was wondering if Dahlia woke up and got any dinner. Or if she woke up and moved to the bed where she'd be more comfortable. Or if she'd fed her cats.

Her *cats*.

Mikey was thinking about her cats.

When he should've been soaking up all the attention from fourteen ladies who would've each loved to give him a different place to stay tonight.

He took a swig off his Bud Light and then winked at one of the two blondes to his right. "And if you think that's bad, wait till you hear about the time our stage almost collapsed."

They all oohed and squealed and begged for more, and Mikey gave it to them.

But forty-five minutes later, having bought them each one last drink, he turned and waved down the little redhead tending bar. "Check please, sweet pea."

Because he might've looked in his element, but he didn't have the stamina to keep it up another couple of hours.

Fighting decreased lung capacity thanks to standing outside watching that fire burn too long last night, he told himself. Or maybe feeling the effects of too many days in the bitter cold Northern winter.

"You sick?" Little Red said. "Or are you heading over to the karaoke bar?"

No room to be offended. Little Red's sister Saffron had played fiddle and backup guitar with Will's band for a lot of years. No doubt Little Red had heard plenty of stories. He winked at her, then leaned further over the bar and lowered his voice. "You been here long?"

"Since last July."

"You know the Milked Duck lady?"

"Dahlia? Yeah. She patched my nephew up after he took a tumble in the park last fall. And she volunteers at the shelter all the time. She has the sweetest guinea pig. Have you met him? He's *adorable*."

Yep. Everybody loved Dahlia. "Haven't had the pleasure. Heard she had a boyfriend a while back. You know anything about that?"

Little Red's eyes narrowed. "Why?"

"Asking for Billy. Thought we heard the guy knew his way around a keyboard, and we might could have some use for him," Mikey lied.

Little Red shrugged. "Don't know anything about him."

"Not even a name?"

"Oh, well, yeah. I know his *name*."

She peered at him expectantly.

Yep, everybody wanted something. And he was being a big ol' dummy caring, but he wanted to know who'd cheated Dahlia out of her money.

So he could track him down and pound the guy into the ground.

Wasn't right. Hadn't felt like doing that since Mari Belle announced she was getting divorced.

Mikey reached into his wallet and pulled out an extra twenty.

"I don't want a big tip, you dolt," Little Red scoffed. "I want to know every trick Saffron ever played on you guys when she was touring with you. I could use a new idea or two this year. Need to get back my family prankster crown. And, you know, avoid Saffron getting the better of me now that she's living close and all."

First time all night Mikey felt a real smile on his face. "You're the baby of the family, right?"

"I prefer to think of it as the best," Little Red said.

Exactly like Saffron would've said about her own position in their big family. "Name now, list of pranks tomorrow," he said. "Maybe this weekend, if you want everything. Billy might remember a few things I forget."

She grabbed a napkin and scribbled something, then clapped it into his hand. "Deal. And if you don't follow through…"

"Trouble like I ain't ever seen," Mikey finished for her. He had a notion he'd seen some of that trouble from Saffron on the road. Usually funny, unless it was aimed at him. "Got it."

Little Red gave him a sassy wink. "And this stays between us."

"Every last word," he agreed.

Because if anyone found out Mikey had gone to the trouble to find out a girl's ex-boyfriend's name, he might have to face what wanting the information really meant.

And he didn't know what bothered him more—that he cared, or that she wouldn't care that he cared.

Because Mikey Diamond was a lot of things, but an upstanding, follow-through kind of guy for a woman he barely knew wasn't one of them.

Especially a woman who was only using him to get to *Billy*.

Life was craptastic like that sometimes.

The sound of a key scraping a lock jolted Dahlia out of a sound sleep. Parrot dug her claws into Dahlia's leg and flung herself away, except she didn't make it. Instead, she tumbled in a ball of fluff, caught up in the blanket she was pulling off Dahlia, bringing a chill to Dahlia's skin. Sam shot out from his perch at her feet, and Dean growled low behind her.

The room was dark, save for the soft glow from the light in Hank's cage in the kitchen. The front door swung open. Cold air swirled into the room. A tall dark figure clomped inside.

"Freeze," Dahlia said. "Show me your hands."

Because all she had on her side was the element of surprise.

"Holy shit, Dahlia, it's me," a familiar voice said.

"Oh. Right." She helped Parrot untangle from the blanket, then pulled it back up to her chin.

Wait.

She hadn't gotten herself a blanket.

Which meant—"You're a nice guy sometimes," she blurted.

He snorted. "Yeah, I'm a prince."

Dahlia ignored the stomping and grumbling. "What time is it?"

"Bedtime."

For once, there wasn't a hint of suggestion in his voice. She watched his shadow track toward the bedrooms. "Are you sick?" she asked.

His shadow stopped, and even in the dark, she could feel his flat, not-amused gaze. "No."

Dahlia's belly grumbled. She huddled into herself in her chair. Obviously not best time to ask if he'd brought pizza. And it made her mad that she wanted more to ask if she'd done something to offend him.

He wasn't hers.

He wasn't her *problem*, she corrected herself.

His problems weren't her problems.

He stopped in the doorway to the short hallway leading back to the bedrooms and reached up to hook his fingers on the frame. "You get dinner?" he asked.

A little gruffly, but still.

He'd asked.

"I'm fine."

He snorted again. "Right."

That did it. She pushed to her feet and hit the light. He squinted. She did too, but she also poked a finger in his direction. "I *am* fine," she said. "I might be an idiot when it comes to men, but I'm fine, and you looking down your pointy, warty nose at me won't change that."

He touched the tip of his smeller. "Warty?"

She wished. And it wasn't pointy either. It was actually a very nice nose. Straight. Distinguished. With a small scar on the bridge that she'd noticed while he was in The Milked Duck earlier. "I was speaking metaphorically. And you know what else? When I *do* have relationships with men, I don't simply eat them like candy. I take the time to get to know them. To *savor* them. To *appreciate* them. Because they're human beings, and all human beings deserve respect."

His Adam's apple bobbed, and his gray eyes had gone dark. "Even the ones who go and steal all your money?" he said.

"They don't *steal*. I give it to them. Because people are priceless. Money's just paper."

"Necessary paper."

"I make do. You use having it as an excuse to be a man-whore."

His eyes went darker and his cheek twitched. "For the record," he said smoothly, "I was a man-whore before I made it big."

"Before *Billy* made it big."

"Before *I* made it big." He crossed the carpet, slow as a panther and every bit as deadly. "*I* write half of Billy's songs. *I* got a touring gig before the world had a clue who *Billy* was. *I* sent money home to my momma before *he* finally pulled his head out of his ass over that damn divorce lawyer here. Hell, I kept him alive. Don't tell me I don't know what people are worth."

He was right in front of her now, a seething mass of solid,

offended male. Subtle scents of beer and frost and new leather wafted off him, and the storm rolling in his eyes made the pit of Dahlia's belly squeeze.

She should've asked about the divorce lawyer, kept him talking about Billy, but she was trapped between Mikey and the chair, and she didn't mind nearly as much as she should've. She put her hands on his chest to push him away, but the act of pushing was harder than it should've been.

Perhaps because his chest was harder than she wanted it to be.

Her fingers lingered on the soft, warm fabric of the cotton T-shirt beneath his open jacket. "My bad," she said, all breathless, brainless female.

Just as she was anytime anything with a penis and a pulse showed any signs of needing saving.

Usually, they didn't need saving from *her* though.

"Yeah," Mikey said, his voice huskier and lower than it had been a minute ago. "Your bad."

There was still a glimmer of insulted ego turning his lips down, but his dilated pupils were aimed at *her* lips, and he made no move to push her away.

She needed to back up before she really stepped in it. Because Mikey didn't *need* anything from her. He didn't *want* anything from her.

Nothing he couldn't get from any other willing, able-bodied female anywhere else in the world.

"Sorry," she stammered.

His eyebrows nodded.

His *eyebrows*.

The man was so freaking cocky he could use his *eyebrows* to make her feel like a heel. She shoved his chest.

"You know what? Never mind. I'm *not* sorry. Because you *do* walk around acting like you're some kind of cosmic gift to the female population of the world, and I don't want to be one of them anymore."

"You don't want to be a woman?"

She shoved him again, because he hadn't even budged the first time. "I don't want to be one of your simpering hussies. Or anybody's sucker. I want to be a nice person who helps people who legitimately need help. Is that so much to ask?"

"In this world? Yep."

"Would it kill you to be optimistic?"

He tilted his head. Scratched his cheek. Then nodded with his freaking *eyebrows* again. "Probably."

She wanted to shake him. To give him a shot of happy to combat the grumpies he was carrying around. And she wanted to shake herself for wanting to fix his grumpies. His grumpies were not her problem. *"Argh."*

One side of his lips quirked up in a sexy smirk. "Got a cure for that frustration you got going on," he said.

"Got a cure for your ego?"

His eyes narrowed thoughtfully, and it hadn't escaped her notice that he was happier now than he'd been when he walked in. As if she'd made him happy by insulting him and picking a fight with him.

She'd never been a giver like *that* before.

Perhaps it was because his dang ego enjoyed winning a fight too much.

"You know," he said slowly, "I just might."

And before she could fully backtrack to remembering that they were trying to cure his ego, he lowered his face to hers, brushed her cheek with his nose, and then suckled her bottom lip into his mouth.

A jolt of sheer feminine need shot between her thighs the same time a squeak caught in her throat.

There was a hint of cold to his lips and his fingers when he tangled them in her hair, but the rest of him radiated hotter than a fire. And ducks help her, she didn't push him away again.

She may have fisted his shirt and yanked him closer. Or possibly parted her lips and kissed him back. It all got a little fuzzy.

A little fuzzy, and a lot *holy yowzers*.

If they weren't careful, they'd set her house on fire too. Spontaneous kiss combustion. And if he could set every nerve ending she owned up in flames simply by kissing her, she'd probably explode if either of them shed any clothing.

She whimpered.

The sex with Ted hadn't been as good as this kiss.

Mikey eased out of the kiss, his chest rising and falling rapidly against hers. "Nope," he said. "Didn't work."

"Didn't...?" she panted.

"Cure my ego." His grin spread across his lips, but didn't wipe the vulnerability sneaking into his gray eyes. "Might could be we need to move this to the bedroom to work it out better."

Her thighs clenched against the rising swell of need aching at the very heart of her womanhood. "You're hopeless."

"So save me, Dahlia." He followed the murmur with a gentle nip at her ear, and she all but melted on the spot.

"I hate you," she whispered.

Because he knew her weakness. He was using it against her. Shamelessly.

And she didn't care.

"Yeah," he murmured. "I kinda hate me too."

And he dropped his hands and turned away and retreated to his bedroom, where he clicked the lock. Loudly.

Her knees gave way, and she sank back into her chair.

Mikey Diamond didn't need saving.

Dahlia did. From him.

5

*M*ikey was up with the sun the next morning. Never was his favorite time of day, but he'd heard the damn cats yowling, and he'd guessed that meant Dahlia was awake.

Good thing there wasn't anybody around to see him tripping over his own two feet to get out of the bedroom before she left for work.

Kissing her hadn't been his plan last night—his dreams, yes, but his plans, no—but she made him do it. She drove him crazy, and kissing her was the only way he figured he could've won that argument.

Huh.

He was getting better at lying to himself too.

He made it into the kitchen in time to see her setting out three separate bowls of cat food. One canned, one dry, one a mix of the first two. She loved on the black and orange cat on the counter, then bent to put the dry food on the floor, giving him a spectacular view of her perfectly curvy, jean-clad backside. The grey cat pounced on the dry food, but she pushed him away with a white socked foot, then bent again and set the mixed food in front of him.

Crazy cat lady had a whole routine for getting each of her cats fed.

"Good boy, Dean," she cooed. "That's my sweet patient kitty, Sam. Here you go, Parrot, love."

Mikey swallowed hard.

Wouldn't have minded having her spoon-feed him some cheese grits and talk to him like that.

"Don't step on Marvin," she said without turning around.

Mikey looked down and yelped.

There was an itty-bitty cat rolling at his feet.

No, not a cat.

A freaking guinea pig.

"He's next, then I'll scramble some eggs," Dahlia said.

"And wash your hands between?" Mikey prompted.

The look she gave him could've competed with one or two of Mari Belle's favorites. Surprised she didn't give a big ol' sigh to go along with it. "No need. The cats already licked the pan for me."

He sucked in a disgusted breath, and her dimpled grin brightened the whole room. "Too easy, *sweet pea*," she said. She pointed to the coffeepot. "Full strength if you need it. And I'm guessing you do."

He needed something, and it wasn't anything he'd ever known he needed before. But the coffee was a good start, so he poured himself a cup—after he rinsed it out plenty good—and then got out of her way while she fed the guinea pig and moved on to whipping up some eggs.

"Been thinking," Mikey said. "You make pretty good ice cream, and I like to eat ice cream. You're short on money, I've done pretty well for myself. What you need is a business partner."

She cracked an egg so hard on the counter, it exploded yolky goo all over her hand.

"And maybe a keeper," Mikey added.

That nastygram she sent him with her eyes could've exploded another egg all on its own. "I do not," she said crisply, "need a partner, nor do I need a *keeper*."

He eyed the egg splatter on the counter.

"And that one's yours," she said.

"C'mon, Dahlia," he said.

Her shoulders bunched. Just because he said her name.

Was he that much of a jerk?

"I don't need to be rescued." She grabbed a long string of paper towels and attacked the egg mess.

"Working on getting your money back from your ex?"

She didn't answer. Instead, she swiped harder at the egg, chasing the mess across the counter.

"Ain't such a bad idea, letting me help you out," Mikey said. "Come next month, we're off on tour. Most likely won't even have to see me again. Won't get up in your business, so long as you're not giving handouts to the next guy what comes along—"

"No."

"Though I ain't saying you would. Then you can know where your pets' next meals are coming from, and I can know you ain't out there selling God-knows-what next—"

"I said *no*. And I meant no. Capital N, capital O. No-way-in-*hell* no."

Mikey stared at her over his coffee. What was wrong with his idea? "Ain't like I'm asking you to sleep with me to get it," he said. "Just offering. Like friends."

"Friends." She shifted her shoulders toward him, her anger brewing hotter than the coffee and messier than that there egg. "Are we *friends*?"

Mikey didn't have much experience in real relationships with women, but even he could see this wasn't going where it was supposed to go. "Sure, sweet pea. We're friends."

"*Friends* do not kiss and then go lock themselves in separate bedrooms."

"They do if they want to stay friends."

Unless he was reading this wrong—which was a pretty decent possibility, all things considered—she'd just silently called him the biggest moron to ever walk out among mere mortal morons.

Huh.

Ain't anybody ever called him that before. Not even Mari Belle, and she was pretty darned good with the silent insults.

"We're not friends," Dahlia said. She snatched a spatula out of a drawer and then slammed it shut. "In case there was any doubt."

"We might could be," he said.

Partly because he could see a possibility of Dahlia being one of his few close female friends—Mari Belle and Will's Aunt Jessie and her psychic being the other three—and partly because he knew it would irritate Dahlia, and irritating her seemed the smarter choice than kissing her again.

And he was definitely getting ideas about kissing her again. Solved their arguing right quick last night.

"Do you have any idea why I don't want your money?" she snapped.

"Can't even begin to imagine," he said honestly.

"And *that*"—she poked the spatula in the air at him—"is why we will *never* be friends." She slammed the spatula down. "You know what? Make your own damn eggs."

She stopped to scoop up the guinea pig, then one cat, then a second cat—how, he couldn't explain, as she still only had two hands, but she pulled it off with flair—then nudged the third cat on out the door, a picture of hot indignation.

And danged if Mikey wasn't stiff as a lead pipe.

She didn't want him.

First woman he'd met in months—years—*ever*—who wasn't Mari Belle that he had more than a passing curiosity about, and she didn't want him.

This friendship-with-girls crap was for the birds.

THE PROBLEM with running a public ice cream shop was that anyone could come in during open hours, and for the next few days, Mikey did.

Every. Day.

Twice on Friday, and the second time, he brought along his guitar and sat there and plucked at the strings, writing things down, using straws to tap on the table. She couldn't kick him out—word leaked around town that Billy Brenton's hot-as-sin drummer liked to hang out at The Milked Duck, and suddenly eighty-four million single women needed ice cream.

On a subfreezing January day.

And he sat there and flirted with Every. Last. Woman.

Right there.

In Dahlia's shop.

He'd left a twenty tucked into her freezer where the Chocolate Orgasm prototype had been, and then another twenty tucked in where she found a missing sample of her Cherry Popper yesterday.

And he'd had a steak dinner waiting for her when she got home last night too. Complete with candles and crème brulee cupcakes. To thank her for her hospitality, he'd said.

Also to thank her for her hospitality, he'd folded her laundry. Including her underwear.

He'd touched and folded her underwear.

Her *underwear*.

At least, she thought he had. She'd found no evidence that he was having guests during the day while she was working and he *wasn't* at The Milked Duck, but with the way he flirted so shamelessly when he was in her shop, she wouldn't have put it past him.

Aside from seeing him at the shop and the steak dinner, she'd mastered the art of avoiding him. She left for work before he was up in the morning, and then took her dinner into her bedroom and ate it in bed while she read.

She needed to ask him how much longer he needed a place to stay, but that would've involved talking to him, and she didn't want to talk to him.

Because when she talked to him, she let herself believe that all his charm was real. That he truly was interested in her as a person, and that the only reason he flirted with everyone in The Milked Duck was to keep business up for her. That he didn't have any ulterior motives for getting to know her and wanting to stay here. In her house. With her.

He hadn't offered again to help her out financially, which was good. But he hadn't left either. And she thought—or perhaps simply wanted to believe—that he truly didn't understand why his offer was insulting.

She didn't need *money*. Well, aside from food and rent money. She'd kept The Milked Duck because she loved it. She loved making ice cream, loved coming up with new flavors, loved watching the cream and milk and eggs and sugar go from being their own separate substances to transforming into one creamy, delicious treat that could be served so many ways.

She loved that ice cream was universal. That it made people smile on bad days, that a simple cone could bring utter joy to a child, that she provided comfort food to the world.

Mikey didn't understand what any of that meant.

If her sister or parents came to town tomorrow and offered her a loan, Dahlia probably would've taken it. Because her family understood what it meant to spread joy too. And since they were busy spreading their own joy, none of them would be stopping in Bliss tomorrow with cash in hand to bail her out, even if they had it.

Mikey simply thought Dahlia was a fool, and by extension probably her whole family, and that he was doing her a favor.

The ice cream truck song rang out from the front of The Milked Duck. Dahlia's jaw clenched. Mikey hadn't been in yet today, which meant—

Yep.

It meant he was here now. One week from the tasting.

"Afternoon, sweet pea," he said, exactly as he had every other day. He strolled right up to the counter, all lanky grace and annoyingly confident swagger, a hoodie covering all but the bill of his ever-present ball cap, and that leather jacket over all of it. "Don't suppose you need a taste tester for that Sin on a Stick you're serving next week?"

A young mother with a toddler whipped her head toward them from her seat in the corner.

"You are sin on a stick," Dahlia muttered.

"Billy's looking forward to coming." Mikey plopped two bills on the counter. "Asked me to get us both tickets."

Dahlia's heart thudded to her toes. "B-Billy's coming?" she squeaked.

"Suppose that depends on how good these adult flavors are." Mikey winked, prompting Dahlia to process the other meaning of *coming*.

The woman in the corner covered her toddler's ears, but she leaned closer, listening.

Heat flooded Dahlia's face. "That's not what I meant and you know it," she hissed.

Mikey's grin was completely unrepentant. He rocked back on his heels. "Told him he'd be doing me a mighty big favor. Lucky you, he owes me a favor or three."

Holy ducks.

Billy Brenton was coming—making an appearance at Dahlia's Risqué Flavor Tasting.

"And he's—and you're—and should I—"

"You leave all the details to me, sweet pea," Mikey said.

She wanted to hug him.

She wanted to leap over the counter and throw her arms around him and squeal and thank him and hug him and kiss him.

Because this—*this* was so much better than giving her money. This was helping her earn it herself rather than taking a handout. Having Billy Brenton show up was a handout in its own way, but still.

It meant more than money that Mikey asked Billy for her.

Maybe he did get it. Maybe he cared in his own way, and he was slow to show it. Maybe—

The ice cream truck song rang out again, and a tall, slender brunette with either one hell of a great head of hair or the best stylist in the world walked in the door. She slid her sunglasses off, loosened her ivory knit scarf, and narrowed her sights on Mikey.

Who promptly left his money sitting on the counter and beelined to her. "Hey, sweet pea." He wrapped her in a hug, then pressed a kiss to her cheek. "How is it that you look even better today than you did in September?"

She patted his cheek, then returned the welcome kiss. "You are my absolute favorite person. Have I mentioned that lately?"

He put his hand to the small of her back and steered her to a table. "Hey, Dahlia, a couple Cookies 'N' Creams over here. In waffle bowls."

Dahlia's belly rolled like it was freezing a sour batch.

She never learned, did she? Mikey Diamond didn't need her.

He had a hundred million other put-together floozies at his disposal.

She scooped out two large servings of Cookies 'N' Cream, dumped them into waffle bowls, and then overcharged him. For both the ice cream and the tickets.

He didn't blink.

He was too busy laughing with his newest *sweet pea*.

Dahlia stormed back to the back, blinking back tears. Which was utterly ridiculous, because things were looking up for The Milked Duck. Billy Brenton was coming to her adults-only tasting. She'd leak that out on Facebook and Twitter, and then all she'd have to worry about was making enough ice cream and not exceeding the shop's capacity.

And *then* she could worry about getting Mikey Diamond out of her life. Out of her life, out of her head, out of her heart.

Forever.

MIKEY HAD GOTTEN twenty-nine phone numbers since arriving in Bliss, and he had zero interest in using any of them.

Were it not for the fact that his dick twitched every time he caught a whiff of ice cream, he would've worried about himself.

Worried more, that was. He was plenty concerned that his attention span for one woman had exceeded his previous record for an infatuation with a woman who wasn't Mari Belle by a good five days. But he definitely wasn't having any performance anxiety concerns.

So when Dahlia still hadn't left her bedroom by lunchtime Sunday, the one day of the week The Milked Duck was closed, he took it upon himself to get to know his hostess better.

Purely in the interest of getting close enough to kiss her again.

He knocked on the door.

Then knocked again. And this time, he waited.

But he still had to knock a third time before the door flung open.

"What?" Dahlia said.

Mikey clamped down on the urge to say what he really wanted—he was far from a genius about women, but he had a notion Dahlia wouldn't appreciate *Wanted to see if you wanted to make out*—and instead, went against every instinct he had. "Do you sing?" he asked.

She blinked. "What?"

"Been writing songs with Will—with *Billy*—since we were kids, but I don't sing. He always covers that part. But I got this song I've been working on, and I need to hear it out loud. And"—he held his hands out—"I don't sing."

Her head tilted, and the tips of her red-streaked hair brushed one shoulder. "You—you need me to sing?"

He nodded.

She used both hands to push her hair back while she looked down at the floor and toed the carpet. "I'm more of a shower singer," she said shyly.

Which was the darned most adorable thing he'd seen all day.

Adorable.

Mikey didn't do *adorable*.

"Me too," he said. "Between the two of us, we might could almost make it sound better than if your cats sang it."

She lifted her face to him and pushed her glasses up her nose, a new light growing in her pretty eyes. "I can probably do a *little* better than that."

He grinned back at her. "Then let's hear it."

She nodded. "Okay."

He pulled a folding chair he'd dug out of the garage into the living room for her, not all that optimistic about the song itself, but feeling pretty dang good that she was out here. With him. With a real smile blooming on those lips.

And turned out she could read music. Could laugh at herself when she hit a sour note, could laugh at him when he picked the wrong chord on the guitar—was a reason he preferred sitting at a drum kit. And she gave him what for over some of the lyrics she said were disrespectful to all of womankind, which she didn't suppose a guy like him cared about.

He didn't tell her he put the lyrics in to get a rise out of her. She glowed when she got good and spun up. Sight to behold right there.

Been a long time since Mikey laughed so much over a song. And danged if Dahlia didn't turn a shade prettier every single minute. Even the minutes she was chewing out his ass.

So he changed a few more lyrics until he had to rename the song "Dahlia," and watch her trip and giggle every time she tried to sing her own name until she finally tossed all the papers in the air. "I'm calling uncle," she declared. "You're not really going to use this song."

"Better than anything else we got for the next album," he told her. "God's honest truth. Bet you a dollar Will puts this one in."

Her nose wrinkled. "You call Billy *Will*."

"Who he is. Wasn't Billy until his first manager suggested a stage name."

"Are you two fighting about the fire? Is that why you're not writing with him today?"

Mikey's shoulders bunched. He wasn't ever the guy in the direct spotlight, but he'd learned not to say the wrong things to the wrong people. Got back eventually, and Will's team didn't much like cleaning up messes. Didn't happen a lot—Will was one of the good guys, and in most parts of his life, Mikey tried to be too—but nobody was perfect, and public opinion was fickle.

Still, this was Dahlia. And Will being Will, he'd blown off Mikey's apologies over the fire, said it wasn't anybody's fault, and they'd both had most of their focus on writing new songs for the next album.

But only most of their focus. And Mikey still didn't like where the rest of Will's focus was going. "How much do you know about that divorce lawyer chick from here?" he asked Dahlia.

She went stiff. "Lindsey? Not much. She grew up in Bliss, went to college, came home, and now she kinda does her own thing over in Willow Glen. Why?"

Her cheeks had gone rosy again, her words stilted.

Like she was hiding something.

"What else?" Mikey said.

"I'm not from around here. That's all I know."

Mikey propped an arm over his guitar and looked at her.

She stared back.

With cheeks so rosy they looked as though they had lava flowing under them, and her fingers fidgeting like she wanted to pick at her nails.

Mikey lifted an eyebrow.

"Well, if nobody else has told you, *I'm* not going to," Dahlia said.

Mikey shoved to his feet. "If she hurts Will again, I'll—"

He'd what? He didn't make commitments to women, but he didn't threaten them either. And he wasn't real big on not being able to do anything.

And it pissed him off like nobody's business that he couldn't protect Will from being a dumbass about her. *Again.*

Mari Belle needed to get her pretty little ass up here yesterday.

"Will?" Dahlia's cheeks crinkled. "This is about Billy? I thought you meant—" She clamped her mouth shut.

"Thought I meant what?"

Her pulse fluttered at the base of her neck. She pulled her legs into her chest and hugged them. "You said *again*," she said. "Why did you say *again*? And why would Lindsey hurt him?"

"You first, sweet pea," he ground out. "What do you know?"

Dahlia's pupils dilated. Her lips twitched, but she sealed them tight.

"What did she say?" Mikey pressed.

Dahlia shook her head.

Mikey drummed his fingers on the guitar. Lindsey's messing with Will sucked donkey eggs. Lindsey's messing with Mikey wasn't going to happen. Crazy as it was, the divorce lawyer lady had a thing for matchmaking on the side. And Will bought into it. Almost made Mikey feel normal about his own relationships—but hell if Mikey would let his own love life be her business.

"She say something about me?" he said. Because he was starting to get the feeling Dahlia didn't give a horse's patoot about Will.

"You first," she said. "What's your problem with Lindsey?"

This was why Mikey didn't do relationships with women. They got all emotional and couldn't answer a simple question without making demands in return. "Ain't really none of your business," he said.

She shrugged. "If you say so."

And there she went, doing that *I know something you don't know* thing. Like it was a trump card.

Aw, *hell*.

"She go and tell you we're a good match?" he said. Damn meddling woman. She'd been there that time Mikey met Dahlia before the fire.

Dahlia's eyelashes twitched. She hugged her legs tighter. "If I heard that rumor," she said, "that *would* make your problem with her my business, wouldn't it?"

"Nope."

"Then it doesn't matter what she did or didn't say about you or me or anyone else, because you're too stubborn and self-absorbed to consider the possibility that you could make someone else happy by letting her make you happy too, despite the very reason we might be together." She unfolded herself from the chair and stood. "Good luck with your song."

He blinked at her retreating backside. "Wait a minute. What the hell, Dahlia?"

"It doesn't matter," she repeated, still walking away. "You, obviously, are not in a place to consider a serious relationship with anyone other than yourself. I can't fix you if you don't want to be fixed, and I shouldn't want to. I've learned my lesson."

And while Mikey stood there feeling like he'd taken a right hook to the gut, which didn't make much sense since *she* wasn't making any sense, she snagged her coat from the coat closet, then slipped on her shoes.

He took two steps toward her. She was leaving. He didn't even know if he had her, and he was losing her. "Where are you going?"

"The shelter. Because real animals know how to show a girl some love."

The door clicked shut behind her, leaving Mikey not only confused, but confused and lonely.

He really needed to fix that. If only he could figure out how.

6

*D*ahlia was beginning to hate the sight of her house. She sat outside in her car, the temperature inside dropping as quickly as the light was fading from the evening sky, staring past the bare brown elm branches at the warm glow coming through the living room curtains.

The empty, burnt shell of Mikey's former rental house was still a gaping hole in the neighborhood. Tonight it gave her chills from thinking about how lucky he'd been to not be inside sleeping when the fire started.

She hadn't actually heard anything about anyone speculating on her relationship—or whatever it was—with Mikey, but the rumors said Lindsey *knew* that sort of thing. And Dahlia had thought that maybe if Mikey had heard something, it might give her some clue as to why he'd gotten under her skin.

And if he liked her back, or if he was just amusing himself with her.

If he liked her enough to not care who did or didn't think they'd make a good couple.

She watched her breath crystallize over the steering wheel. A few snowflakes drifted down from the rapidly darkening sky.

Mikey wasn't a bad guy. Under all the innuendos and the swagger, he had a sweet side.

He hid it well, but it was there.

She could bring it out of him. He wasn't asking for money, he didn't need her to watch his pet, nor did he truly need *her* house to stay at. There was nothing about him that screamed *user*.

He simply needed to be loved.

No, *she* thought that's what he needed. What he thought he needed, she had no idea. Men were so complicated.

Her front door opened, and the man himself stepped out into the flurries in the fading evening light. He was in a jersey-style black and gray Henley, jeans that did all the right things for his lean hips and long legs, cowboy boots, and the ever-present Billy Brenton ball cap over his shaved head.

Smokin' hot, put together, and edgy on the outside, hiding a wounded soul in need of saving on the inside.

She dropped her head to the steering wheel.

He'd be even worse than Ted. Because what he took wouldn't be something replaceable like money.

Mikey knocked on the car window. She rolled her head to the side and popped open one eyeball. His hands thrust deep into his pockets, and he fidgeted on his feet.

The longer she sat here, the colder they would both get. She, at least, had a coat.

She reached for the door handle.

He must've taken that as a sign, because he grabbed the handle from the outside and pulled her door open quicker than she could finish herself. "Nice afternoon?" he asked.

His voice was warm and rich, with no hint of innuendo or hidden agenda. Like hot chocolate without the marshmallows, because the hot chocolate had finally figured out it was pretty spectacular on its own and didn't need the extra filler.

Yep, Dahlia had a problem.

He offered a hand, and even though she was perfectly capable of climbing out of the car herself, she took it. "It was," she said.

She stood and pocketed her keys.

Mikey didn't drop her other hand. Instead, he studied her, eyes shadowed beneath the brim of his cap.

Her pulse kicked up.

"Will and Mari Belle saved me," he said. "From myself. I was a hell of a kid. My daddy worked hard, my momma did her best and spent most of my childhood taking care of my sick grandmama, but I wanted to have fun. Being friends with Will, having Mari Belle fussing over both of us—they got me out of a lot of trouble. Kept me from finding even more. And now I'm watching him do the dumbest thing he's ever done. This time he knows better, and I want to stop him, but I can't. Can't anybody else either."

Despite the freezing temperatures outside, everything inside Dahlia went soft and melty.

He *did* have a sweet side.

"Mari Belle?" Dahlia said.

Mikey winced, but there was something more there too. Something sad. "His sister. She'd hit this place like a hurricane. Saw it all go down the first time, when Will met her."

"Lindsey."

"Yeah."

Dahlia had speculated as much while she was playing with the kitties at the shelter all afternoon.

"She broke him," Mikey said. "Met on some spring break trip. Made him think she was falling in love with him, then dumped his ass hard. He wasn't the same after that. Not for a long, long time." He slid her a look. "You watch a friend get that tore up over a girl, makes you think twice about not letting yourself be dumb enough to care about somebody who's gonna let you down."

She didn't know why he was telling her this, but her heart went sappy-gooey at the thought that he might think Dahlia was special enough to risk getting hurt over.

She squeezed his fingers. "You can't find the real highs if you don't risk the hard falls."

"Breaking a bone, getting scraped up, having a finger freeze off, that don't scare me." He tapped his chest. "But this ol' heart? It ain't so tough."

"It wouldn't work as well if it were."

His lips hitched into a lopsided half-grin. "Can't say I ain't real suspicious of Lindsey's motives. Don't have any need of her butting in on my love life. But you—you're special on your own. No matter what she did or didn't say."

"I didn't really hear anything. If that helps at all. And you're pretty special too."

A snowflake landed on her nose.

And Mikey—tough, swaggering, womanizing Mikey—bent to kiss it.

Dahlia's heart swelled. Warmth glowed in her chest and chased away the winter cold. She tilted her head up, and his mouth captured her lips.

He dropped her hand to wrap his arm around her, his other hand fisting in her hair. She clutched his shirt and hung on, felt his skin vibrating beneath the thin fabric, the cold of the air, the brush of snowflakes on her skin making his touch even hotter.

His kiss was searing and deep and desperate, as though he needed to kiss her more than he needed to breathe.

It was quite possible she too needed him to kiss her more than she needed to breathe.

He tugged on her. "Inside?" he moaned into her mouth.

"Mm-hmm." Because when he kissed her and touched her and *needed* her, nothing else mattered.

And it was time she let herself need him too.

IF MIKEY HAD THOUGHT STUMBLING upon a sleeping Dahlia in an arm chair was a special kind of precious, it had nothing on watching a naked sleeping Dahlia in the dim light of dawn.

He was usually a sneak-out-of-the-room-an-hour-later type guy, but he was also usually fooling around with women who liked him only because he played in a big-name band. Women who expected him to sneak out.

Felt so... hollow, now.

Empty.

Like maybe Dahlia was right. Maybe he did need saving.

Parrot trilled out a funny sound in her sleep and stretched, shoving at Mikey's knee. The cat had been between the two of them since they'd both collapsed in an exhausted, sexually satisfied heap. Dean was curled up beside Dahlia's shoulder, and Sam was crouched on Mikey's pillow.

Waiting to pounce if he did anything to Miss Dahlia, for sure.

Even the guinea pig was making *don't screw with my momma* glares at Mikey from its perch in its cage.

Mikey needed to figure out what he was going to do about that.

Because all his life, the only woman he'd ever wanted, *wanted* wanted, had been out of reach. And now—now, he had another one, completely different, sneaking into his heart.

He hadn't told her the whole truth about why he didn't let people in—the part about Mari Belle. But what he'd said about watching Will get all tore up—that had been true for a long time too. Might be time Mikey was ready to let Mari Belle go.

Felt better than he ever thought it could.

Dahlia made a little noise like Parrot's.

That big ol' useless organ in Mikey's chest ka-thumped like a bass drum.

She bunched her shoulders up to her ears and lifted her arms over her head with another contented sigh, then slowly blinked open those big ol' seas of blue. "Hi," she said shyly, her eyes not entirely focused, but beautiful without the obstruction of her glasses.

Mikey suddenly understood what his fellow songwriters meant when they talked about a woman's smile putting a melody in their heads. Because that simple syllable in her sweet little voice had inspired a symphony's worth of arrangements.

He stroked her silky hair and smiled back. "Hey."

He pushed the cats out of the way, rolled her onto her back, and showed her exactly how happy he was to see her this morning.

If her giggles and shrieks that turned to moans and gasps were any indication, she was just as happy to see him.

Mikey Diamond might've been the kind of guy to fall in love after all.

THE MILKED DUCK WAS EMPTY, save for Dahlia's two part-time helpers, but they were all rushing around, anticipating the first guests for her Risqué Flavor Tasting event any moment now.

The up front freezers were stocked with Chocolate Orgasm, Peachy Passion, Sexual Favors, Mikey's favorite Cherry Popper and more. She had a case of Sin on a Stick treats ready to go and a temporary menu up on the board behind her. After word had gotten out that Billy Brenton would be stopping by, she'd sold out of tickets.

She'd also prepped a case of pints of various flavors in case anyone wanted to take some home.

Mikey kept insisting he'd buy all of them, usually with suggestions of which of her body parts he'd lick the ice cream from, but she'd already had to wash ice cream out of her sheets twice this week.

She smiled to herself and put her cool fingers to her warming cheeks.

This had been a *very* good week.

And not just for her body.

Mikey Diamond had a sweet side that was utterly impossible for a girl to resist, and he topped it off with being so *not* needy that Dahlia couldn't quite believe he was real. In fact, she'd even coerced a confession out of him that he'd spent all those days flirting with women in her shop just to bring in business.

And it had worked.

Sales were already up enough that she could pay her rent this month.

The ice cream truck song rang out. She adjusted her Milked Duck apron, checked that her two assistants were ready, and then smiled at the first of her guests coming in from the dark, cold evening. Soon, the coatracks in the corners were full, conversation drowned out the doorbell tune, and sample cups were being passed around, along with speculation about the secret ingredient that made Sexual Favors the early favorite in the crowd.

There was also speculation about when Billy Brenton might arrive.

Dahlia, though, was more curious about when Mikey would arrive. She didn't know if he were one of those fashionably late people, or if he'd gotten tied up working on a song, or if—or if he'd simply gotten everything he wanted from her already.

How a person could get tired of laughing so much with someone else wasn't something she could understand. Or how someone could whisper so many secrets and confide so much in another person and then decide it wasn't worth it anymore.

She shook off her doubts and handed over another sample of Chocolate Orgasm. She needed to slip away and check her phone. Just for a second. In case—

A waft of cold air swept through the room, quickly followed by gasps and whispers.

There he was, all tall grace and easy movements, still in his ever-present ball cap. She didn't need to see Will—funny how Dahlia thought of him as Mikey's friend now, even though she'd probably have a heart attack and a half if Will knew her name—to know he was with Mikey. The shift in energy in the room said as much.

Mikey's gaze landed on hers, and Dahlia smiled.

Let everyone else fuss over *Billy*. Dahlia had a different idea of what made a guy a rock star.

Mikey smiled back, soft and goofy, and Dahlia's heart did the same thing it had been doing all week—it thudded to the floor with a happy, whimpering sigh.

She was in it deep this time.

He said something to Will, and the two of them moved through the crowd toward the counter.

No, wait—not two of them.

Three of them.

Mikey leaned over the counter to kiss her on the cheek. "Hey, sweet pea. Nice party." He nudged his friend. "Billy, this here's Dahlia. She might could solve some of your problems if you take some of her ice cream home."

Will turned a soft brown-eyed smile on Dahlia. His well-groomed stubble made him look rugged, and his red plaid button-down open over his white T-shirt was classic Billy. "Real pleasure, Miss Dahlia."

She shook his hand without turning into a slobbering mass of *Ohmigod, I love your songs*—which would've been a no-brainer two weeks ago—and then offered Mikey a saucy smile instead. "I don't know, Mikey. He's so hot, it would melt before he got it home."

A feminine laugh startled her. "Oh, I could like you," the third member of their party said.

Mikey's cheeks went a tad pink. "Dahlia, meet Mari Belle."

Mari Belle. Will's sister.

Dahlia had heard a good bit about Mari Belle this week too.

She was pretty—perfect makeup, perfect golden brown hair, perfect way of using her hazel eyes to make a simple Bliss girl feel as though she'd been sized up. Dahlia shook her hand as well. "Nice to meet you," Dahlia said.

"Likewise."

Her Southern accent was less pronounced, her words more polished than the guys'. But suddenly Dahlia was thinking about

Mikey's old tales of Mari Belle keeping him and Will in line, memories of all the things the three of them had done together.

She'd been his first crush, he'd admitted.

What he hadn't said was that she still was, or that she'd be here tonight. In Bliss. In Dahlia's ice cream shop.

Mikey had his hand at the small of Mari Belle's back, his body angled so he was closer to her than he was to Will, and he probably didn't even realize he was doing it, but his gaze kept flicking back and forth between Dahlia and Mari Belle.

Not Dahlia and Will, his best buddy.

Dahlia and his best buddy's big sister.

A chill touched the pit of Dahlia's stomach. She turned to Will. "How lovely to have a visit from family while you're here."

"That's what she tells me," Will said with a wink. But there was a grimace lurking in there too, as though it wasn't the treat it was supposed to be.

"Do you have brothers?" Mari Belle asked Dahlia.

She shook her head.

"Doesn't matter how old they get, they still need watching after." Mari Belle's smile was pleasant, her expression warming, but Mikey had spilled a few other details about Will's private life this week, and more than once Mikey had mentioned that Mari Belle would be more dangerous than a tornado if she decided to do something herself about knocking some sense into her brother. So it was no surprise that both she and Will looked a little tense.

But it didn't explain Mikey being so high-strung.

He hadn't even made a joke about anyone sampling Sin on a Stick.

"Ice cream?" Dahlia said. She held on to her smile, but frost was spreading through her midsection. "You can pick and choose, or I can set you up with a tray of one of each."

"Ice cream would be right good, sweet pea," Mikey said. He nudged Mari Belle. "Ain't had real pleasure in your mouth until you've had Dahlia's Sexual Favors."

Will ducked his head and coughed. Mari Belle's eyes bulged.

Dahlia's skin erupted in mortification. "The ice cream flavor," she said quickly. She pointed to the menu. "The Peachy Passion is really good too, though Mikey's probably not getting any tonight."

Mikey flashed an almost normal grin at her. "Any...?"

"*Any*," she said, with the right emphasis for him to take that every way he and his dirty mind possibly could.

She snagged two full trays of samples and passed them across the counter to Will and Mari Belle with a bright smile and an "Enjoy!" then dug out a Sin on a Stick and shoved it at Mikey. "And here's your phallisicle."

He looked down at the chocolate-covered banana treat.

Then back at Dahlia.

Then the slow grin started, the one that began with the right corner of his mouth going up, then traveled across his lips until the left corner joined in. His lips parted, adding some tooth to the smile. "Looks delicious, sweet pea," he said.

And then in a blink, he leaned across the counter, slanted that smile over her mouth, and kissed the ever-loving ducks out of her.

Right there in her ice cream shop, full-on with tongue, his hands tangled in her hair and his thumbs brushing her supersensitive ears. While people around them tasted Chocolate Orgasm and Sexual Favors, and then whistled and cheered.

It wasn't until he broke the kiss that she realized she'd dropped the Sin on a Stick and was clutching the lapels of his jacket.

"But not as delicious as that," he said with a wicked Mikey grin. He picked up the chocolate-coated, marshmallow ice cream–stuffed banana and saluted her with it, then shot a glance at Mari Belle.

The frost that had melted in Dahlia's midsection solidified into ice.

He didn't need money from her. He didn't need a lifetime supply of ice cream. He didn't need her connections at the shelter.

He needed her to make Mari Belle jealous.

"Smile for the interwebs, Mikey," Will said. He and Mikey turned in sync, their backs to her, and Will held up his phone. "You too, Miss Dahlia," Will drawled.

Holy *ducks*. She smiled automatically, watching herself on the screen between the latest man to dangle her heart over a cliff and the superstar who was saving her shop.

She watched her round cheeks that spoke of too much sampling of the ice cream, her glasses, her eyes too big and wide, her lipstick smeared off.

Will snapped the photo, then murmured something to Mari Belle.

Mari Belle, the utter picture of put-together Southern perfection. And not, according to Mikey, because she lived off her brother's coat-tails, but because she had a solid job and a life and had made something of herself all on her own.

No wonder Mikey loved her.

Mari Belle drifted into the crowd, getting a few curious glances while her brother charmed Dahlia's guests. Will sampled her ice cream, gesturing to it while he smiled, Mikey by his side diffusing some of the attention and being his own confident, smooth, but undeservedly overlooked self.

And while Mikey and Will made the rounds, Dahlia kept serving samples and taking orders for take-home containers and answering that yes, the risqué flavors would be available off the secret adults-only menu all winter long.

Tonight's tasting was everything she'd needed it to be. On a professional level.

"You make all your own recipes?" Mari Belle asked, suddenly next to the counter again. She had finished her samples.

"Some were my aunt's that I modified, but others are completely original." Dahlia forced another smile. It wasn't Mari Belle's fault—exactly—that Mikey had been in love with her since the dawn of time.

"This Chocolate Orgasm is the best chocolate ice cream I've ever had."

"Mikey helped with that one," Dahlia heard herself say.

Mari Belle laughed, a light, pretty sound. "I sense his influence in the Hazel's Nuts."

Dahlia nodded, even though her heart was getting heavier and heavier. "Completely his idea."

"Classic Mikey," Mari Belle said on a chuckle.

"Dirty old man in training."

"If you think he's bad now, you should've known him when he was fifteen." She cast an affectionate smile in the men's direction. "He's a good guy underneath it all."

"He is," Dahlia agreed softly. "And he doesn't know it."

Mari Belle turned a sweet smile Dahlia's way. "I'm glad *something* good has come of their being here."

As if Dahlia was the *good*. But Dahlia didn't feel good. She felt insignificant and frumpy beside Mari Belle.

"They won't stay much longer," Mari Belle said, which echoed what Mikey had told Dahlia earlier. Bliss had been pretty understanding of Will's presence, but people were snapping pictures. And if Will had posted his own selfie, there was a very good chance The Milked Duck would soon be overrun.

Which was sort of exactly the point.

As if on cue, Will glanced their way and gave Mari Belle a nod.

Mikey glanced their way too and winked at Dahlia.

"We're going to need one of every flavor to go," Mari Belle said. She slid a hundred dollar bill onto the counter. "And don't argue about keeping the change."

"But I—"

Mari Belle held a finger to her lips and pinned Dahlia with a commanding kind of look that could've made a three-year-old snap to attention and salute. Dahlia swallowed the rest of her argument. "I'll get a bag," she corrected herself.

When she got back to the counter with the to-go bag, Mikey and Will had made it back. They both grinned at her, and Will peeked inside. "You're a peach, Miss Dahlia. Don't suppose I might could talk you into a carton of S'mores ice cream to go too? One of my favorites right there."

It was Lindsey's favorite flavor, Dahlia knew. And by the way

Mari Belle's placid expression wavered toward frustration, and the way Mikey rubbed his eyes, they suspected as much too.

Dahlia kept a straight face—or tried to, anyway—and sent one of her helpers to the back to fetch it. "Anything else?"

"Depends. You ship? Danged good ice cream. Might could use some of that on the road this summer."

The Milked Duck, official ice cream supplier for Billy Brenton's *Hitched* tour. Dahlia gulped back a squeal. "Absolutely." A little dry ice, some overnight shipping, and they'd be golden.

Will flashed her a smile that was killer in its own right. "Add in some of them cupcakes from the bakery around the corner, and I'm thinking Bliss has everything a man needs. Ain't that right, Mikey?"

"Can't go wrong here," Mikey agreed. But his gaze slid to Mari Belle before landing on Dahlia, and her poor frosted heart cramped.

Dahlia's helper reappeared with the S'mores ice cream, and Dahlia put it in the bag. "Thank you so much for coming," she said. To her utter mortification, she felt tears welling in her eyes. Mikey and Will —they'd boosted her ticket sales for tonight and probably her ice cream sales for the rest of the winter. Two superstars helping little old her.

Will reached across the counter and grabbed her in a hug. "Know a little bit about hard times, darlin'," he said. "Besides, ain't every day I get to help out a girl who's got ol' Mikey so smittened. Never thought I'd live to see the day." He pressed a friendly kiss to her cheek, his whiskers tickling, then let her go. "Thanks for a nice evenin', Miss Dahlia." He tipped his hat. Mikey grinned at her again and grabbed the ice cream bag, and Mari Belle smiled too. "Nice to meet you, Dahlia. Hope we'll see you again."

The three of them headed out of The Milked Duck, Mikey saying something to Mari Belle that made her laugh, and Dahlia's whole heart collapsed in on herself.

They had probably saved her shop.

But she'd discovered there *was* something that meant more to her than The Milked Duck. Something she cared about as much—maybe even more—than her pets.

And even though she'd thought he could be hers, she was wrong.

He pushed the door open with his back, smiled at Mari Belle when she passed by, made what was undoubtedly a crude joke to Will, and then the door swung shut behind them and they disappeared into the chilly evening.

And even though she was inside in the warm, lit room, she felt as though her soul had gone somewhere darker and colder than even an Illinois winter night.

7

When Dahlia didn't answer her cell phone for the third time, Mikey turned from pacing her empty living room and grabbed his coat. He would help her clean up, chase out the last of her customers, and then see if she'd give him a private tour of The Milked Duck's kitchen.

And by *private tour*, he meant *naked ice cream tasting tour*.

Before he made it to the front door, it opened, and Dahlia came in. She looked as though she'd gone wrestling with a wild hog in a pit filled with ice cream, and she was still a darned pretty sight. "Hey, there, sweet pea. Good night?"

Her bright blue eyes were dull and sad, and when he approached her for a hug, her shoulders bunched up and she stepped away. "Yeah," she said shortly. "Thank you."

He blinked.

He hadn't ever been the sharpest arrow in the set when it came to women, but he was plenty good at knowing how it felt to be used.

But this was *Dahlia*.

She hadn't—she wouldn't have—would she?

"What's up, sweet pea?" he said.

She lifted her face so she was looking him right in the eye. "You knew Mari Belle was coming tonight."

Some *uh-oh* filtered into his brain, followed quickly by the normal dread inspired by a jealous woman. "Uh, yeah."

"She's nice," Dahlia said.

"Yeah," Mikey said again. Because even a dummy like him knew better than to put many more syllables into his answers right about now.

"You didn't mention that you're still in love with her."

Mikey's jaw hit his chest. "I—you—we—"

I'm not was all he had to say. He wasn't in love with Mari Belle anymore. He had Dahlia now, and she liked him back, and that was that.

Except he apparently didn't have Dahlia.

And his denial was stuck somewhere below his throat and above his heart, choking him in a place he couldn't scratch.

"Did it work?" Dahlia said. Her voice wobbled. "Did you make her jealous?"

"I wasn't—she didn't—*Dammit*, Dahlia, stop it."

"I am such a sucker," she muttered.

One of them was a sucker, but he was pretty sure it wasn't her. "Yeah, you got what you wanted, and now you're cooking up a story about my best friend's sister so you can get rid of me."

Dahlia's eyes pinched, but she didn't back down. "Do you love her?"

"She doesn't love me," he said, his heart talking even though his head was hollering at him to shut the ever-loving hell up. "She never has, and she doesn't know how I feel—*felt*—so it don't matter a hill of beans."

"Loving isn't about getting," Dahlia said. "It's not about being loved back. It's about giving yourself to someone else with no expectation of ever getting it back."

"Then what the hell's this about?" He gestured between them.

"Because this sounds an awful damn lot like me getting attacked. Ain't very *loving*."

A tear dropped onto her cheek, and Mikey had to fight an insane desire to wipe it away and kiss her silly.

She was being ridiculous. Utterly ridiculous.

"I do love you," she whispered. "But I can't save you. I'll never be her. I'll never be what you really want. And I love *me* enough to know that I deserve to be more than a consolation prize."

His gut was twisting into knots, his heart howling. She couldn't do this. She couldn't leave him dangling, believing she didn't want him because she thought he was still holding out hope Mari Belle would notice him.

Or was this a convenient way to shove him out of her life now that he'd delivered Will to save her ice cream tasting tonight?

She'd done well. She'd done really, really well tonight. "You're not a *prize*," he bit off.

Best he could do.

She snorted out a humorless laugh. "Obviously."

"You're *you*, Dahlia. And I thought that was someone special."

"But not special enough," she said softly. "Not the right special for you."

Mikey fisted his hands and shoved them in his pockets. "What the hell do I have to say to prove to you that you're wrong?"

"Answer the question, Mikey. Do you still love Mari Belle?"

"*Yes*." Hell and tarnation. "No," he corrected.

But it was too late. Her eyes crinkled up, her breath came out loud and soggy.

Cripes, now he had crying Dahlia. That was worse than mad Dahlia, because she wasn't supposed to cry. She was supposed to laugh and sass him and keep him in his place.

"No, I don't," he said, and he meant to say it stronger, but truth was, he couldn't be sure he didn't.

Seeing her again today made him feel ten years younger. Made him wonder what might've been. Even with all the time he'd spent with Dahlia, all the fun they'd had, all the ways she made him feel warm and good and whipped on the inside, he'd still looked at Mari Belle and wondered what life would've been like if she'd known he loved her when she got married all those years ago. If she'd known he loved her when she got divorced. If she knew now he still thought about her.

"I think you should go now," Dahlia said quietly. "Thank you. For everything."

"Dahlia, wait—"

But she trudged out of the room, three cats on her heels, Dean sending Mikey the feline version of the stink-eye.

Rightfully so.

Because this one was all Mikey's fault.

MARI BELLE HAD her light-brown hair down and makeup off when Mikey knocked on her hotel door an hour later. She was in sweatpants, a UGA sweatshirt and bare feet.

Usually a woman's bare feet made his dick twitch, but not even her hand on his elbow got a reaction out of his body. "Hey," she said. She stepped out of the room and eased the door shut. "Everything okay?"

"I ever tell you I loved you?" he said.

The words felt foreign and thick and wrong, but he had to say them. To taste them.

To see if Dahlia was right.

Mari Belle lifted a perfectly plucked brow, a smile playing on her lips. "Drunk on ice cream?" she said lightly.

He glared at her, and her smile slipped.

"Sure," she said. "You and Will both. Remember the time I drove to Nashville from Pensacola because you called and said you had a gig at The Bluebird, but it turned out to be The Bluebeard, and you two got skunk-ass drunk and I hauled your butts off for coffee and cold showers? There was lots of love going on that night."

"For real," Mikey said. "Did I ever tell you I loved you for real?"

She heaved one of them Mari Belle sighs she did so well and slumped back against the wall. "Mikey, sweetie, you've never done *love*."

If Dahlia had said that to him, he would've been insulted. Because she *knew* he was capable of love. "I did," he said. "I loved you."

"Problems with the girl?" she asked quietly.

Mikey stared down the hallway at the rows and rows of hotel doors. Wasn't much different than any other hotel he'd stayed in countless other nights of his life on the road. Smelled the same, like pool water and overbaked linens and well-trod carpet, with a hint of whatever flowery shampoo Mari Belle used tossed on top.

An iron brick sat in his stomach.

Wasn't the life he loved anymore.

"Think she used me to get Will to bring in publicity for her ice cream," he said, but that didn't feel right either.

"Dahlia?" Mari Belle said.

Mikey nodded. Couldn't look at her, couldn't hardly make his neck move the right way, but he forced it.

"That girl adores you," she said. "She had Billy Brenton standing right in front of her, and she couldn't take her eyes off *you*."

Yeah. He'd noticed.

"Kiss me," Mari Belle said suddenly.

Mikey's head jerked up.

"Go on." Mari Belle settled her hands on his shoulders. "Kiss me. Make mad, passionate love to me, Mikey Diamond."

He didn't move. Not a single cell in him reacted to her words and her touch. Might've been because she put as much feeling behind the words *mad, passionate love* as a turnip could've done.

Or maybe he'd only been in love with who he thought she was all these years. "Quit being an ass," he said.

"I'm fixin' to tell your momma you said that," she murmured, and it was definitely more seductive, but it still did exactly zilch for him.

"C'mon, Mikey," she said. "Show me how you feel."

She was completely serious now, none of her smart-ass showing.

And the funniest thing happened.

Mikey opened his eyes, and he *saw* her.

She wasn't his Mari Belle. She was Will's sister, screwed up in all her own ways, capable of loving him back like a brother, but incapable of giving him more.

She was a good lady—a good mom, a good sister, a good friend—but she wasn't the girl of his dreams.

"Thanks, MB." He pressed a quick kiss to her cheek. "You're a peach."

"Happy to help," she said. "Good luck digging yourself out of that hole. I liked her."

Mikey scratched at his hat. "Yeah," he said. "Me too."

Mari Belle flashed an impish grin. "Go get her, tiger." And then she let herself back into her room, leaving him alone to figure out his mess all on his own.

TUESDAY MORNING, Dahlia and her weepy heart were finishing up feeding the cats when someone knocked on her door. Her feet leapt into action even as her brain advised caution.

It might not be Mikey. And even if it was, Dahlia would never be Mari Belle.

Still, she couldn't help herself. Hope sprang eternal. She flung the door open, bracing herself.

But nothing could prepare her for the sight of Mikey's brunette from the ice cream shop and her firm grip on the collar of a blonde-haired, blue-eyed, shamefaced Ted Lummings. "Ms. Mallard," the brunette said, "I believe this man has something that belongs to you."

Dahlia's bruised heart launched itself into an unsteady rhythm.

"Um, hey, Dahlia," Ted said.

Dahlia couldn't find words. She simply looked between the brunette and Ted.

The brunette gave his collar a shake.

Ted wiped his brow, his cheeks an unflattering shade of pink, his breath coming in quick puffs of clouds in the cold morning. "My business took off," he said, his words stilted, eyes wincing, "so I have your share of the profits to give to you."

"He's offered to go with you to the bank to make sure the transfer goes through to your account," the brunette said. "You know how it is, sometimes numbers get transposed and suddenly you're waiting on money to come in from a bank account that doesn't exist. Right, Ted?"

He visibly gulped. "Um, yeah."

"Who—" Dahlia swallowed the lump swelling in her throat. "Who are you?" she asked the brunette.

"Friend of a friend." She winked. "Heard a lot about you. And then I just happened to run into this guy, and he knew you too. What a coincidence, right?"

Dahlia's eyes stung. She had no idea where Mikey had found this woman, but there was no doubt he'd hired her to solve Dahlia's problem.

"Thank you," she whispered.

The brunette nodded. "The bank? I believe it's on your way to work."

Dahlia shook her head. "I don't want the money."

She didn't. It was a lesson she'd learned the hard way, and while she'd caught a lucky break to survive this winter, she didn't want to have the reminder of her mistakes sitting in her bank account.

She'd keep the smarts, and perhaps one day she'd make a similar mistake again for a good cause, but it was just money.

Ted blew out a breath. "See?" he said to the brunette.

She slanted her brows at him, and he shut up.

"I want my profits donated to the local animal shelter," Dahlia said.

Ted's face went pale. All but the two bright pink stains on his cherub cheeks.

"You have access to their bank account to verify the transaction?" the brunette said.

"I'll make a phone call."

The brunette smiled. "We'll wait here."

Dahlia swiped at her eyes and smiled back. "If you see—you know who—will you tell him thank you for me?"

"Honey, if you don't find that man and thank him yourself, then you're not half the woman I hoped you would be." She gave Ted's collar a shake. "Time's wasting, Ms. Mallard. You have ice cream to sell."

She did.

But after they made the trek to the bank with the shelter's accounts manager, she had something more important to do than selling ice cream.

———

WITH THE MYSTERIOUS brunette's guidance, Dahlia tracked Mikey down at a pretty two-story yellow house in a newer neighborhood in Willow Glen, a trendy little city half an hour from Bliss. Mikey's rental truck was in the driveway, but until the door swung open, she wasn't entirely sure she was in the right place.

But there he was, her strong, handsome, perfectly imperfect savior-wannabe.

He peered at her cautiously, then opened the door wider. "Hey, sweet pea. Come on in." A guitar echoed inside, and Dahlia realized she'd stumbled upon the house where Will had been hiding out since the fire.

She wanted to launch herself at Mikey. To properly thank him for his help. For his friendship.

For just being *him*.

But she wrapped her arms around herself instead of hugging him. "Your, ah, *friend* brought Ted and my, erm, *profits* by this morning. Thank you."

He scuffed a toe on the light-colored rug covering the oak floors and nodded. "Yeah. Anytime."

"The Bliss animal shelter was very grateful."

His grin popped out. "You're one of a kind, Miss Dahlia."

The tune coming from the guitar in back changed, and Dahlia recognized the melody.

Her face warmed, and she put her hands to her cheeks.

Billy Brenton was playing the song she'd helped Mikey write. The one he'd named after her.

"I tried to kiss Mari Belle," Mikey said.

Three sour notes rang out from the back room. Dahlia went back to hugging herself, tighter this time.

"I couldn't do it," he rushed on. "Because she's not you."

Dahlia's breath caught in her throat. "You—"

"You were right Saturday night. I thought if she saw me serious with someone, she might realize I could be more than a family friend." He tilted his head and offered a self-deprecating smile. "And more than just a man-whore."

Dahlia wanted to shake him. "You were always more than just a man-whore."

His grin was coming back, more real. "She left Sunday, but I don't miss her. I miss you. I miss your cats and your big, open living room floor and your jokes and your ice cream freezer and the way you can fry an egg with your eyes when you're mad and your big heart." A real Mikey grin made an appearance. "And your Sexual Favors," he added softly.

Dahlia giggled despite herself. He angled closer.

"I was wrong too," she said. "I was looking for a reason to push you away. Because you scare me."

He stopped.

"You scare me because you make me feel good about being me. Even the sucker parts. And I'm so afraid that if I let myself love you, that you'll take something more than my money or my good intentions. That you might honestly take my heart. And that can't be replaced."

"If it helps," he said, "I can give you a backup. Thought I was missing mine, but it just walked in the door with you."

She shuffled closer to him, inhaled his fresh, clean, male scent. "And you're leaving next month," she said.

He looked back toward the sound of the guitar. "Always loved life on the road," he said quietly. "Felt more like home than home did. But home—been a long time since I've been this kind of home. Been where I belong."

Her heart was stuttering out a hopeful rhythm. "Where do you belong?"

"Right here, sweet pea." He brushed a hand over her hair, slid her glasses back up her nose. "With the only woman in the world better than all the rest put together."

"I'm not—"

"Was talking about Parrot," he said.

Dahlia's head jerked all the way up, and Mikey lowered his smiling mouth to hers. "Thinking I'd be getting the better end of the deal here," he said against her lips.

"You definitely would," she agreed.

But she had her arms around him, and he was doing things to her lips that were probably illegal back in Pickleberry Springs. And what he was doing with his hands *definitely* was—she'd looked up a few laws last week—and she couldn't ever remember laughing while she kissed a man before, but she couldn't ever imagine kissing anyone else, ever again.

She pulled back from his kiss. "I'm sorry I didn't trust you."

"I earned that one," he said. He kissed the tip of her nose and smudged her glasses. "And I'm gonna spend the rest of my life making sure you know *you* are the only woman I will ever love. And on my honor, I ain't ever tasting another woman's sexual favors. Even if the bakery offers 'em up in a cupcake wrapper and calls 'em whipped dreams."

Dahlia giggled again. "I love you, Mikey Diamond."

"I love you too, my Dahlia. Even if you got here too soon for my big ol' plan to play in Bliss's Battle of the Boyfriends to win your heart here in a couple weeks."

Now *that* was too much. Because Dahlia had never been the kind of girl a guy would've publicly declared for.

Thank the holy ducks for Bliss and its fun traditions, or she still might not be. "I can pretend this didn't happen," she offered.

"Suppose I can too, so long as I get to move back in with you and have me some of your Cherry Popper every night."

"And Chocolate Orgasms?"

"And then some."

"Some...?"

Mikey laughed. "Oh yeah. *Some.*"

She pushed up on her tiptoes to taste his lips again.

Because being smittened with Mikey Diamond was way better than any ice cream.

THE END.

ABOUT THE AUTHOR

Jamie Farrell is the alter ego for *USA Today* Bestselling romantic comedy author Pippa Grant. She believes love, laughter, and bacon are the most powerful forces in the universe. When she's not writing, she's raising her three hilariously unpredictable children with her real-life hero.

Visit Jamie's website at:
www.JamieFarrellBooks.com

THE COMPLETE JAMIE FARRELL
BOOK LIST

The Misfit Brides Series

Blissed

Matched

Smittened

Sugared

Merried

Spiced

Unhitched

The Officers' Ex-Wives Club Series

Her Rebel Heart

Southern Fried Blues

JAMIE FARRELL'S PIPPA GRANT TITLES:

The Girl Band Series

Mister McHottie

Stud in the Stacks

Rockaway Bride

The Hero and the Hacktivist

The Thrusters Hockey Series

The Pilot and the Puck-Up

Royally Pucked

Beauty and the Beefcake

Charming as Puck

I Pucking Love You

The Bro Code Series

Flirting with the Frenemy

America's Geekheart

Liar, Liar, Hearts on Fire

The Hot Mess and the Heartthrob

Copper Valley Fireballs Series

Jock Blocked

Real Fake Love

The Grumpy Player Next Door

Standalones

Master Baker *(Bro Code Spin-Off)*

Hot Heir *(Royally Pucked Spin-Off)*

Exes and Ho Ho Hos

The Bluewater Billionaires Series

The Price of Scandal by Lucy Score

The Mogul and the Muscle by Claire Kingsley

Wild Open Hearts by Kathryn Nolan

Crazy for Loving You by Pippa Grant

Co-Written with Lili Valente

Hosed

Hammered

Hitched

Humbugged

Printed in the USA
CPSIA information can be obtained
at www.ICGtesting.com
CBHW021557300624
10899CB00013B/340

9 781955 930031